LAST
BREATH

Other Books by Brandilyn Collins

Rayne Tour series

1 | *Always Watching*

2 | *Last Breath*

3 | *Final Touch*

Books for adults

Dark Pursuit

Exposure

Kanner Lake Series

1 | *Violet Dawn*

2 | *Coral Moon*

3 | *Crimson Eve*

4 | *Amber Morn*

Hidden Faces Series

1 | *Brink of Death*

2 | *Stain of Guilt*

3 | *Dead of Night*

4 | *Web of Lies*

Chelsea Adams Series

1 | *Eyes of Elisha*

2 | *Dread Champion*

Bradleyville Series

1 | *Cast a Road Before Me*

2 | *Color the Sidewalk for Me*

3 | *Capture the Wind for Me*

Brandilyn Collins & Amberly Collins

LAST BREATH

BOOK TWO

the Rayne Tour

ZONDERVAN®

For Mark Collins, best husband and father in the world.

ZONDERVAN

Last Breath
Copyright © 2009 by Brandilyn Collins

This title is also available as a Zondervan ebook.
Visit www.zondervan.com/ebooks.

Requests for information should be addressed to:
Zondervan, 3900 *Sparks Dr. SE, Grand Rapids, Michigan 49546*

This edition: ISBN-978-0-310-74896-0

Library of Congress Cataloging-in-Publication Data

Last breath / Brandilyn and Amberly Collins.
     p. cm. — (Rayne Tour series ; bk. 2)
     Summary: For sixteen-year-old Shayley, a dying man's last words about her long-lost father are almost worse than the violence and murders occurring during her famous mother's rock concert tour, and she is driven to find out if they are true.
     ISBN 978-0-310-71540-5 (softcover)
     [1. Murder—Fiction. 2. Fathers and daughters—Fiction. 3. Paparazzi—Fiction. 4. Single-parent families—Fiction. 5. Rock groups—Fiction. 6. Fame—Fiction. 7. Mystery and detective stories.] I. Collins, Amberly. II. Title.
PZ7.C692Las 2009
[Fic]—dc22
                                               2009015212

Published in association with the literary agency of Alive Communications, Inc., 7680 Goddard Street, Suite 200, Colorado Springs, CO 80920. www.alivecommunications.com

Interior design: Christine Orejuela-Winkelman

Printed in the United States of America

15 16 17 18 19 20 21 22 /DCI/ 20 19 18 17 16 15 14 13 12 11 10 9 8 7 6 5 4 3 2 1

Dear Reader,

Glad to see you back for more of Shaley O'Connor's story. This sequel picks up right where the last one left off—at the concert in Denver's Pepsi Center. If you haven't read book one in the series, *Always Watching*, do that first! You've missed a lot of excitement.

Imagine a burning question in your life, a huge black hole you want to fill. That's how Shaley feels about her unknown father. Who is he? Where is he? Did he really do what he's been accused of?

It's time for Shaley to start learning some answers.

We'd love to hear from you after you've read the book. If you drop by our website at *www.brandilyncollins.com*, you can email us from there.

~ *Brandilyn and Amberly Collins*

PART 1

Sunday 2009

1

Your father sent me.

The last words of a dying man, whispered in my ear.

Were they true? What did they mean?

Guitars blasted the last chord of Rayne's hit song, "Ever Alone," as Mom's voice echoed through the Pepsi Center in Denver. The heavy drum beat thumped in my chest. With a final smash of cymbals, the rock song ended. Multicolored laser lights swept the stadium. Time for intermission.

Wild shrieks from thousands of fans rang in my ears.

I rose from my chair backstage. Tiredly, I smiled at the famous Rayne O'Connor as she strode toward me on high, red heels. In the lights her sequined top shimmered and her blonde hair shone. She walked like a rock star — until she stepped from her fans' sight. Then her posture slumped. Mom's intense blue eyes usually gleamed with the excitement of performing, but now I saw only sadness and exhaustion. How she'd managed to perform tonight, I'd never know. Except that she's strong. A real fighter.

Me? I had to keep fighting too, even though my legs still trembled and I'd probably have nightmares for weeks.

Your father sent me.

I had to find out what those words meant.

"You're a very brave young lady," a Denver detective had told me just a few hours ago. I didn't feel brave then or now.

"You okay, Shaley?" Mom had to shout over the crowd's screams as she hugged me.

I nodded against her shoulder, hanging on tightly until she pulled back.

The applause died down. Voices and footsteps filled the stadium as thousands of people headed for concessions and bathrooms during the break.

Kim, the band's alto singer, laid a tanned hand on my head. A white-blonde strand of hair stuck to the pink gloss on her lips. She brushed it away. "How you doin'?"

"Fine."

Our bodyguards Mick and Wendell walked over to escort Mom. Wendell's eyes were clouded, and his short black hair stuck out all over. He hadn't even bothered to fix it since the life-and-death chase in our hotel a few hours ago. He was usually so picky about his hair. Mick looked sad too. They both had been good friends with Bruce.

Bruce had been killed hours ago. Shot.

And he'd been trying to guard me.

My vision blurred. I blinked hard and looked at the floor.

"Come on." Mom nudged my arm. "We're all meeting in my dressing room."

Mick and Wendell flanked her as she walked away.

Usually we don't have to be so careful backstage. It's a heavily guarded area anyway. But tonight nothing was the same.

Kim and I followed Mom down a long hall to her dressing room. Morrey, Kim's boyfriend and Rayne's drummer, caught up with us. He put a tattoo-covered arm around Kim, her head only reaching his shoulders. Morrey looked at me and winked, but I saw no happiness in it.

Ross Blanke, the band's tour production manager, hustled up to us, along with Stan, the lead guitarist, and Rich, Rayne's bass player. "Hey," Ross put a pudgy hand on Mom's shoulder. "You're doing great." He waved an arm. "All of you, you're just doing great."

"You do what you have to," Stan said grimly. His black face shone with sweat.

We all trudged into the dressing room. Mick and Wendell took up places on each side of the door.

Marshall, the makeup artist and hairstylist, started handing out water bottles. Marshall's in his thirties, with buggy eyes and curly dark hair. His fingers are long and narrow, and he's great with his makeup tools. But until two days ago, he'd been second to Mom's main stylist, Tom.

"Thanks." I took a bottle from Marshall and tried to smile. Didn't work. Just looking at him made me sad, because his presence reminded me of Tom's absence.

Tom, my closest friend on tour, had been murdered two days ago.

Mom, Ross, Rich, and I sank down on the blue couch — one of the furniture pieces Mom requested in every dressing room. This one was extra large, with a high back and thick arms. To our left stood a table with lots of catered food, but no one was hungry. I'd hardly eaten in the last day and a half and knew I should have something. But no way, not now.

Stan, Morrey, and Kim drew up chairs to form a circle.

"All right." Ross sat with his short, fat legs apart, hands on his thighs. The huge diamond ring on his right hand was turned to one side. He straightened it with his pinky finger. "I've checked outside past the guarded area. The zoo's double what it usually is. The news has already hit and every reporter and his brother are waiting for us. Some paparazzi are already there, and others have probably hopped planes and will show up by the time we leave."

Is Cat here? I shuddered. The slinky-looking photographer had pulled a fire alarm in our San Jose hotel the night before just to force us out of our rooms. The police told him not to get within five hundred feet of us. Like he'd care.

My eyes burned, and I was so tired. I slumped down in the couch and laid my head back.

Ross ran a hand through his scraggly brown hair. "Fans out

there are gonna be talking about what they heard on the news before the concert. Rayne, you should say something about it."

"Yeah." Mom sighed.

Rich frowned. He was moving his shaved head from side to side, stretching his neck. His piercing gray eyes looked my way, and his face softened. I looked away.

Everyone was being so nice. Still, it was hard to know three people had died because of me.

Ross scratched his chin. "We got extra coverage from the Denver police at the hotel tonight. Tomorrow we head for Albuquerque. It's close enough for Vance to drive the main bus without a switch-off driver, and the next two venues are close too. But we've all been through a lot. Can you guys keep performing?" He looked around, eyebrows raised.

"Man." Morrey raked back his shoulder-length black hair. "If three deaths in two days aren't enough to make us quit ..." His full lips pressed together.

I glanced hopefully at Mom. *Yeah, let's go home!* I could sleep in my own bed, hide from the paparazzi and reporters, and hang out with my best friend, Brittany.

But canceling concerts would mean losing *a lot* of money. The Rayne tour was supposed to continue another four weeks.

Mom leaned forward, elbows on her knees and one hand to her cheek. Her long red fingernails matched the color of her lips. "I almost lost my daughter tonight." Her voice was tight. "I don't care if I *never* tour again — Shaley's got to be protected, that's the number one thing."

I want you protected too, Mom.

"Absolutely," Morrey said, "but at least the threat to Shaley is gone now that Jerry's dead."

Kim spread her hands. "I don't know what to say. I'm still reeling. We barely had time to talk about any of this before getting on stage tonight. I feel like my mind's gonna explode. And *Tom* ..."

She teared up, and that made me cry. Kim had been like a

mother to Tom. Crazy, funny Tom. It was just so hard to believe he was gone.

I wiped my eyes and looked at my lap.

"Anyway." Kim steadied her voice. "It's so much to deal with. I don't know how we're going to keep up this pace for another month."

Mom looked at Ross. "We can't keep going very long with only Vance to drive the main bus."

Ross nodded. "Until Thursday. I'd have to replace him by then."

"With who?" Mom's voice had an edge.

"I don't know. I'll have to jump on it."

"You can't just 'jump on it.' We need time to thoroughly check the new driver out."

"Rayne." Ross threw her a look. "I *did* check Jerry out. Completely. He had a false ID, remember? That's what the police said. I couldn't have known that."

"You might have known if you'd checked harder."

Ross's face flushed. "I *did*—"

"No you didn't! Or if you did it wasn't good enough!" Mom pushed to her feet and paced a few steps. "Something's mighty wrong if we can't even find out a guy's a convicted felon!"

What? I stiffened. "How do you know that?"

Mom waved a hand in the air. "The police told me just before we left the hotel."

I stared at Mom. "When was he in prison?"

Mom threw a hard look at Ross. "He'd barely gotten out when we hired him."

Heat flushed through my veins. I snapped my gaze toward the floor, Jerry's last words ringing in my head. *Your father sent me.*

My father had purposely sent someone who'd been in prison?

"Rayne," Ross snapped, "I've told you I'm sorry a dozen times—"

"Sorry isn't enough!" Mom whirled toward him. "My daughter was taken hostage. She could have been killed!"

Rich jumped up and put his arms around her. "Come on, Rayne, it's okay now."

Maybe Jerry had lied. Maybe he'd never even met my father.

Mom leaned against Rich, eyes closed. The anger on her face melted into exhaustion. "It's not okay." Mom shook her head. "Tom's dead, Bruce is dead. And Shaley —"

Her words broke off. Mom pulled away from Rich and took a deep breath. "We can't decide this now. It's only fifteen minutes before we have to be back on stage. I still need to change."

Stan stood. "I say we figure on doing Albuquerque, and then we can decide about the rest."

"Yeah, me too." Rich got up, along with everyone else. I could see the business-like attitude settle on all their faces. Soon they had to perform again. Every other concern had to be pushed aside. In the entertainment world the saying was true: *the show must go on.*

Within a minute everyone had left except Mom, Marshall, and me. Mom threw herself into a chair by the bright mirrors so Marshall could adjust her makeup. When he left, she changed into a steel-blue top and skinny-legged black pants.

I sat numbly on the couch, four words running through my mind. *Your father sent me.*

Mom didn't know what Jerry had whispered to me as he died. I needed to tell her. But how? Like me, she was running on empty. It would be one more shock, another scare. I wasn't sure she could take any more and still perform.

Had Jerry told me the truth? Had the father I'd never known — the man my mother refused to talk about — purposely sent a killer to join our tour?

I needed to know. I needed to find out. Because if it *was* true — the danger was far from over.

2

A final encore song, and the concert would be over.

My stomach had started to growl fifteen minutes ago. Not that I could hear it over the music. But I felt it. I'd run to Mom's dressing room and scarfed down sliced meats and cheeses, some pasta salad. My body wasn't quite so weak anymore.

Now for some sleep.

"Thank you, Denver, you've been great!" Mom's voice blared through the arena. The crowd roared back.

"Now," Mom held up a hand, "I need to tell you something."

Everybody kept screaming. It's hard to quiet fans down, especially before an encore.

"Listen up, folks!"

Slowly the noise died down. A few catcalls rang out here and there.

"Thanks." Mom walked down to the edge of the stage. "You all really have been awesome tonight."

More yells. Mom waited them out.

"Okay. I'm sure you all know we've had some trouble the last few days. Tonight, just before the concert, a few more difficult things happened. No doubt you'll be hearing about it on the news when you go home, if you haven't already. We all just want you to know that the band members are fine, my daughter, Shaley, is fine. And that your love and devotion to our music is what keeps us going."

"We love you, Rayne!" a man yelled, and the crowd was off again, screaming.

Mom raised her hand, palm out, for silence. She had to wait a long time.

"The next few days of touring are going to be hard for us. But, as they say, the show must go on. We'd appreciate your prayers."

The fans roared once more.

Prayers? I'd never heard my mom ask anyone for that. But after what we'd lived through in the past two days, I was all for it.

I focused on Carly, my favorite backup singer. An African American with warm eyes and a caring heart, she was the one who'd prayed for me. She was the one who'd told me God was "always watching."

"And now," Mom cried over the noise, "let's have some *music!*"

Stan's guitar struck a chord, and the last song blasted. The fans shrieked.

Ten minutes later, the concert over, Mom and I were back in her dressing room. She looked so tired as we gathered our purses and headed down the hall with Mick and Wendell. Outside, the limos waited to take us to the hotel. Ross had gone ahead and checked us all in. Our suitcases waited for us there, watched over by the bellmen.

From the arena filtered the after-concert sounds of chairs being taken down, the stage being struck. Rayne's own roadies, plus local hired hands, would be at work for hours, packing everything away. Vance would pull out with the bus tonight, along with all the trucks. They'd drive all night and be waiting for us in Albuquerque when we flew in tomorrow.

"Sleep." Mom ran a hand across her forehead as we hit the back private exit. "I just need sleep."

"Yeah. Me too." But she had to be way more tired than I was. At least I didn't have to perform.

Outside, Mom took a deep breath of the night air and put an arm around my shoulder. "You okay, Shaley?"

"I'm fine."

Your father sent me.

The band members, plus back-up singers Carly, Lois, and Melissa, divided into two limos. Tall, skinny Lois hunched down to get into the limo with me and Mom. Carly and Melissa followed.

"Hey, girl, how are you doing?" Carly gave me that wide, easy smile of hers, but her brown eyes searched mine for more than a surface answer.

"I'm doing okay. I just want to get to bed."

Lois shook her head. "Don't we all."

Three Denver police cars escorted us as we headed out of the parking lot, following the lead limo. Up ahead, where our privately guarded area ended, I spotted the paparazzi and reporters. Local security members lined our path, arms out and facing the crowd to keep them back from the cars.

I cringed. Here it came. The cameras, the shouting. Everyone fighting to get around security. I hated it. Especially now. People we knew and loved had been *murdered*. We were still in shock. Why couldn't everyone just leave us alone?

We reached the mob. Flashes glittered the night. Sudden light from movie cameras shot through the window.

"Rayne!" someone yelled. "What happened to Bruce?"

"Why did Jerry shoot him?"

"Why did your bus driver want Shaley?"

"Shaley, talk to us!"

"Tell us about Tom!"

"Shaley! Shaley!"

I scrunched down in my seat and covered my ears. Mom drew me to her chest. "Hang in there, honey. We'll be at the hotel soon. Then nobody's going to bother you."

Until tomorrow when we'd have to go out and do this all over again.

Tears burned my eyes. I longed for Brittany. If only she was still with me. But that very afternoon her mom had insisted she cut her visit short and return home — our tour wasn't a safe place for her to be.

I couldn't really blame a mother for that.

The noise passed. I blinked hard and sat up. Took a deep breath. "Sorry. They just … get to me sometimes."

"After all you've been through?" Carly shook her head. "Little wonder."

Yesterday in a mall Brittany and I had been nearly trampled by reporters and photographers who'd rushed us out of nowhere. Bruce was with us. He'd fought to keep them back.

Bruce. I pictured him lying on the hotel hall floor, blood seeping from his chest and gurgling from his mouth.

Suddenly it all hit — memories of the terror and grief. I leaned back in the seat and closed my eyes, fighting tears.

We needed time to mourn and heal, Mom and me. And we wouldn't get it, not as long as we stayed on tour. It was just go, go, go. Fight the paparazzi. And it would only get worse. The news stories of the murders on our tour would be on every TV station, in every newspaper.

I just wanted to crawl into a cave. But I couldn't. I had to find out about my father.

We pulled into our hotel, following the lead limo. At least here it would be a quick trip up to our rooms, then into bed for me. I couldn't wait to close out the world.

"Oh, no." Mom peered out the window to our right. Her voice dropped low. "They've found us."

No. I leaned toward the glass. Under the shimmering lights of the wide, covered hotel entrance, dozens more reporters, photographers, and camera men milled. The minute we got out of our limo, they'd descend on us like rabid dogs.

Some staff member at the hotel must have talked.

My veins went cold. This was never going to end. Suddenly that walk to the privacy of my room seemed a million miles long.

3

I searched deep inside myself for flecks of energy, sweeping them together into a meager pile.

"Wait." Carly craned her short neck to look out the limo window. "At least I see policemen out there."

"Yeah." Mom sighed. "The manager probably called when they saw this crowd. But it's too little, too late."

Bruce, I thought. We needed him. Two bodyguards weren't enough.

As the first limo edged up and aligned with the door, police and hotel security moved the mob back on both sides. Mick and Wendell got out of the limo door nearest the hotel. The photographers and reporters surged toward them.

Our car waited behind.

"Everybody stay put." Mom's voice was sharp.

Police and security closed in along with Wendell and Mick. The still cameras raised and the red lights of TV cameras glowed. "Stay back!" an officer shouted as Stan and Rich emerged from the limo. The mob yelled and pushed.

Kim and Morrey appeared. The crowd jostled and shouted all the more.

"Shaley, where's Shaley?"

"Where's Rayne?"

"Is it true your bus driver killed Tom and a bodyguard?"

Stan and Rich worked their way toward the wide hotel door. Policemen flanked the door on either side, preventing the crowd from following once they entered. "No!" one of the officers shouted to the reporters. "None of you are going in!"

Raucous voices protested. "It's a free country!"

"You can't keep us out!"

The crowd pushed and yelled, but the policemen stood firm.

Mick and Wendell surrounded Kim and Morrey as they moved toward the hotel. Morrey's tattooed arm was around Kim, but she walked straight-backed and confident, ignoring the chaos.

To our left, other hotel guests were pulling up in their cars to unload, gawking at the scene. Bellmen in bright red uniforms ran around, waving at them to move down farther. One of those bellmen almost got hit by a car going too fast.

In front of us, Mick and Wendell shut the first limo's door. It pulled away.

Our car edged up behind it.

The crowd went wild, shouting my name, Mom's name. Their voices echoed off the portico. Police fought to keep everyone back as our limo door opened.

Mick stuck his head inside. His face was calm, but his jaw was set. "Carly, Lois, Melissa — come out first."

"Shaley!" someone outside screamed.

"Rayne!"

"Shaley, how do you feel about Bruce's death?"

"Is it true your bus driver took you hostage?"

"Will your tour continue?"

Grim-faced, the three women scooted across their seat and exited the car. For a few seconds, the noise outside lulled. They were waiting for me and Mom.

I focused through the tinted glass, looking for the familiar faces we hated. My muscles were tight enough to cramp. "Look." I pointed with a trembling finger. "There's Frog and Vulture." We had nicknames for the paparazzi who hounded us the worst, based on what they looked like. "I don't see — "

I gasped. "Yes, I do! Mom, *Cat's* here!" Fear and indignation shot through me. This guy had just been bailed out of jail. He already faced numerous charges because of the things he'd done to me. And he wasn't supposed to be anywhere *near* us. What would it take to make him stay away?

Mom's expression hardened. "Where?"

At that moment, as if he felt our eyes on him, the ugly, despicable paparazzo we called Cat shot past security and sprinted around the back of the limo. His long, bleached-white hair with two-inch black roots flipped in the breeze as he ran, his gangly arms pumping. In one hand he clutched his ever-present camera.

"How could he *be* here?" Mom's eyes slitted. Her fingers sank into the leather seat, and her teeth clenched. "They told him to stay away from us!" She reached for the door handle next to her. "I've *had* it with this guy."

I grabbed her arm. "What are you doing?"

She shook me off. "I will not have him hounding you *anymore*, Shaley."

Cat reached our side of the car and pressed his face to the window.

Mom cursed and yanked the handle. She threw the door open, forcing Cat backward.

"Mom!"

She jumped from the limo and slammed the door. Cat recovered, swinging up his camera. Mom strode toward him in her high heels, both hands up. "Stop it, *now*!" She grabbed his camera, tore it away, and threw it on the ground.

"Hey!" Cat's face went crimson. He leapt toward the camera.

Mom kicked it away. "You stay away from my daughter!"

Everyone in the mob jerked around. Spotting Mom alone, they surged around the car toward her.

"Rayne!" Mick cried. He started shoving through the crowd.

Carly, Lois, and Melissa reached the hotel door. Wendell left them and came running too.

Cat whirled and faced Mom. "I'll sue you for this!"

"Go right ahead!" Mom jabbed a finger at him. "You'll be doing it from jail!"

Pounding feet surrounded the limo as reporters and paparazzi pushed around it. I whipped my head toward Mom, then back to the right. How far away were Mick and Wendell?

Cat screamed curses, his long arms jerking up and down. Mom yelled back.

"Rayne!" Mick reached the right rear of the limo.

Reporters and paparazzi closed in on Mom, TV cameras rolling.

My whole body flushed hot. Mom needed help! I went for the door handle.

Cat scrambled for his camera. Mom went after him.

I shoved the limo door open. It hit a reporter in the back. He cussed and yanked around toward me. I darted out of the limo.

"Shaley, no!" Mick shouted.

Cat scooped up his camera and twisted back toward Mom. He shook it at her. "I'll be wherever I want!"

"Oh, yeah?"

Mick burst through reporters to my side and shoved me back in the car. "Stay there!" I landed hard, half on the seat, half on the floor. He smashed the door closed.

I pressed my face against the window, looking straight ahead for Mom.

An engine surged.

My focus spun to the left.

A car approached in the loading lane next to ours. Even before it slowed the passenger door was opening, another photographer jumping out.

Cat yelled something. I turned toward him and Mom just as Mick was about to reach them. Cat and Mom were three feet apart. She was shouting at Cat, her back to the approaching car.

Cat's lips pulled into an animal-like grimace. Without warning, he rushed into Mom and knocked her hard. She stumbled.

Brakes squealed.

For those few terrible seconds it all seemed to warp into slow motion. As if in a dream — a nightmare I couldn't stop — my wide eyes saw the car coming, Mom flailing into its path. Mick and Wendell yelling. Photographers turning, aiming their cameras ...

The scene jarred into real time.

Mom's body hit the car with a sickening crunch. The car screeched to a stop. Mom bounced off, sank to the pavement, and lay still.

I shot out of the limo, screaming.

"M om! Mom!"

My voice nearly drowned in all the noise. Chaos swirled around me, people yelling, pushing. Three policemen forced reporters and photographers back. They obeyed as little as possible, their cameras snapping, TV film still rolling. The photographer who'd jumped from the moving car stepped up onto the floorboard of his passenger side door to shoot down at Mom. The driver of the car slipped out his door, pale-faced and shaking.

I saw all of this in a blur. My heart nearly burst from my chest as I fought toward Mom.

Mick and a policeman were kneeling on either side of Mom when I reached her. She was crumpled on her left side, moaning. Another officer posted himself nearby, talking into the radio clipped to his uniform. Calling for an ambulance.

Sobs choked my throat. I flung myself beside Mom, trying to call her name. No sound would come.

"Stand back, Shaley. She needs air." Mick nudged me away. He leaned down. "Rayne? Can you hear me?"

Mom groaned. Her head moved in a tiny nod.

"Okay, good. Help's on its way." He patted her shoulder. "Can you tell me what hurts?"

Mom's eyes fluttered open, then shut. Pain creased her face.

I pressed both hands to my mouth. Every bone in my body shook. *This can't be happening, I can't believe this is happening.*

"Get back!" a policeman shouted.

Kneeling there, hard pavement against my knees, I smelled a dank mixture of dirt and gasoline. My stomach churned.

This isn't happening . . .

I started to fall over. Wendell appeared out of nowhere and caught me.

"It's okay, Shaley, she's going to be okay."

"No, she's n-not. She got *hit*."

"But she's talking, that's a good sign. And the ambulance is coming."

Weakly, I leaned against him, head lolling back. My blurry gaze rose to the crowd of people. They looked on like vultures. Even now — even when a paparazzo had pushed my mom into a *car*, and another paparazzo had *hit* her — even now *every one of the cameras* was rolling, clicking, recording.

White-hot rage shot through my veins. I yanked out of Wendell's arms and shot to my unsteady feet. "Stop it!" My hands waved like a maniac's, my voice so screechy I didn't even recognize it. "*Stop* it, all of you!"

Dozens of cameras turned on me, clicking, filming.

"Shaley, whoa." Wendell pinned my hands to my sides.

I fought wildly. "No, no, let me at them! Where's Cat? Where *is* he?"

A female officer moved in. "We should get her inside."

"No! I'm not leaving my mom!"

"Shaley." Wendell's voice sharpened. "Stop it now. You want to help your mom? This *isn't* helping."

Just like that, all the anger drained out of me. I slumped against Wendell and sobbed.

Kim and Morrey rushed to us, followed by Stan, Rich, and Ross. Kim threw herself down by Mom. "Rayne, honey." She took Mom's hand, leaning over her and rocking. "It's okay. We're here."

More police cars were pulling up. I yelled at the closest officers to find Cat. One of them had already pulled aside the driver who'd hit Mom. But Cat was nowhere to be seen.

Sirens in the distance. The ambulance was coming.

"Move back!" Policemen struggled to clear the lanes for the approaching ambulance. It pulled into the entrance drive and carved through the crowd to a stop some twenty feet behind us. The siren's keen fell away like the last wail of a wounded animal.

Medics spilled out and pushed us back from Mom. Carefully, they turned her on her back. Her chest hurt, she said. Her breaths came short, wheezing. Her face was bruised, a bump bulging on her forehead. One hand hung limp.

The medics loaded her onto a gurney.

"I'm going with her!" I cried.

"No, Shaley." Mick pulled me back. "We'll go in a limo."

"No —"

"It's okay." A young female medic held out a hand to me. "There's room for you, Shaley."

She knows my name, I thought stupidly.

Of course. Everybody knows my name.

Feeling numb, I climbed inside. My mind went fuzzy, like I wasn't really there. Maybe I was asleep — in my own bed at home — and this was just a terrible, horrible nightmare ...

Sitting next to Mom, swaying as the ambulance rounded corners, I held her right hand — the one that wasn't hurt. The siren was so *loud*. Everything seemed too big, too noisy, too bright.

"Mom, I'm here. I love you." I squeezed her hand.

Feebly, she squeezed back.

Did the ride take forever or mere minutes? I didn't know. My brain was filled with such panic over Mom, I had no sense of time. The next thing I remember, the ambulance was surging to a stop.

The back doors flew open. Medics hurried about, pulling Mom out, rushing her through the emergency entrance. I ran after them on weak legs. The first limo slid to a halt behind us. I heard Kim call my name as the doors closed behind me. I didn't stop.

Nurses rushed to meet the gurney, exchanging information with the medics as they wheeled Mom across the floor, around a corner. I moved alongside like a zombie, not wanting Mom out of my sight.

We reached a room. The gurney swept inside. I started to follow.

A nurse stepped in front of me. "You need to wait out there."

"No, I —"

"Yes." She gave me a firm look. "No farther. Stay in the waiting room. We'll come out and give you an update as soon as we can."

The door closed in my face.

5

Alone and shaking, I wandered around the corner.

Kim hurried to me and drew me to her chest. Over her shoulder hung both my and Mom's purses, taken from our limo. Stan, Rich, Morrey, Mick, and Wendell milled behind her, looking around with shocked expressions.

"Come on, hon." Kim leaned her head close to mine. "Let's go sit down. Your mom's going to be all right."

I had no energy to argue, could hardly think. The next thing I knew, all of us were huddled on two yellow couches and some wooden chairs in the waiting area. Kim set the purses on the floor beside me.

Mick and Wendell stayed on their feet, suspiciously watching everyone else in sight. The waiting room was empty except for our group. But if any hospital worker got the bright idea to sidle over for autographs, the two bodyguards stood ready to give them the evil eye.

Police arrived. Paparazzi tried to get inside to film us. Of course. No better footage than trauma — they ate that stuff up.

The officers kept them out.

On the couch, Kim had her arm around me, smoothing my hair.

Carly, Lois, and Melissa arrived in a second limo, along with Ross. He strode across the waiting area toward us as if he owned the place. "Where is she?"

"Around that corner." Stan gestured with his head.

Ross headed that direction like a rolling tank.

The same nurse who'd blocked me stepped into his path. "Sir. You need to stay out here."

"No, I have —"

"Stay out here." Her voice was firm but gentle. "We'll tell you what's going on as soon as we can. Believe me, there's nothing you can do right now, and the doctors need room to work."

Ross turned away from her, his jaw working. He ran a hand across his scalp and pushed back his scraggly hair. "I can't believe this." He started pacing. "I just can't believe this."

Me either, Ross.

The accident had happened so fast. I couldn't process it. One minute my mom was healthy and strong. The next minute she lay like a broken doll on the pavement. The scene played and replayed in my mind. Could I have done something? If I'd gotten out of the car sooner, or kept her from leaving in the first place ...

She'd been trying to protect *me*. I couldn't get over that. She was here, in this hospital, because of *me*.

"Anybody see what happened?" Stan asked.

I pulled away from Kim and straightened. "I did. Cat pushed her. On purpose. He rammed into her."

Gasps rose around our group. Ross pulled up short. "You kidding me? He pushed her into that car?"

"He pushed her, and she stumbled. The car hit her."

Rage and hatred tightened Ross's expression. He leaned forward, weight on one leg, gaping at me. "He'll pay for this. I'll make *sure* that guy's put away."

"Yeah. I'll help you." Rich looked sick.

"We all will," Kim said. She laid a hand on my leg. "Shaley, can you tell us everything you saw, beginning to end?"

Staring at the floor, my voice wooden, I told them. When I was done my throat felt like a desert. Carly pulled a bottle of water out of her large purse and handed it to me. I managed a few sips.

Two officers came to talk to us. One looked about forty, with a wide face and pug nose. The other couldn't be more than twenty-five. He had short brown hair and large eyes the color of chocolate. I caught him gazing at me, and I looked away.

The older one introduced himself as Officer Hanston. He gave me a card with his phone number and I stuck it in my pocket. He and the younger man — Officer Rory — asked questions about what happened, taking notes. The fire of vengeance within me gave me strength to tell my story all over again. "Just put Cat in jail." My mouth twisted, and fresh tears bit my eyes. "I *never* want to see him again."

"Cat — that his real name?" Officer Hanston raised his eyebrows.

I shook my head. "It's just what Mom and I call him. His real name's Len Torret. He works for the tabloid *Cashing In.*"

Ross was still steaming. "I'm going to sue that magazine for everything they're worth. They won't be in business when I get through with them."

"He wasn't even supposed to be near us in the first place." A shudder ran through me. I crossed my arms over my chest. "Detective Furlow in San Jose said they told him not to get within five hundred feet of us because he'd been stalking me. Cat had pulled a fire alarm to force us from our hotel rooms. And he slipped a photo of me into a shopping bag when I was in a crowd at the mall. On the back he wrote 'Always watching.'"

Officer Hanston jotted a note. "Okay. Furlow in San Jose. We'll call him."

A doctor with black hair and a craggy face walked toward us. We all rose to our feet, muscles tense. Awaiting the verdict. My hands were clammy. I wiped them on my jeans.

The doctor's gaze swept our group. "I'm Doctor Devlor. I wanted to give you a report."

"How is she?" Ross demanded.

The doctor held up a hand in a calming gesture. "She'll be okay. She's pretty banged up with lots of bruises. X-rays show three cracked ribs and a broken left wrist. They've just put a cast on that arm. All in all, I'd say she's pretty lucky. Apparently the car that hit her wasn't going too fast. Is that right?"

I rubbed my forehead. "It was slowing to a stop. But a paparazzo was in it, and his driver was coming too fast for a drop-off area. He just wanted to get there and take pictures." My throat tightened. I hated those paparazzi, all of them. "Wh-what do you do for cracked ribs?"

Dr. Devlor gave me a little smile. "You're Shaley?"

I nodded.

"She's been asking about you. The nurses told her you had plenty of people around you."

Tears welled in my eyes. Hit by a car, and Mom was thinking of me.

"To answer your question — we've taped up her chest. She shows no signs of breathing problems or any internal injuries, so that's good. But cracked ribs are a slow heal, and there's significant pain. Just about every movement connects to those chest muscles."

Ross made a sound in his throat. "How long does she need to stay?"

"Two or three days. We've put her on pain meds. When she's able to travel, she can go home. But that's ... where?"

"Southern California."

The doctor tilted his head. "That's a distance. We'll just have to wait and see when she's up to that."

I bit my lip. "Can I see her now?"

"Sure." Dr. Devlor looked around apologetically. "I can't let you all in — there's not enough room. But you should be able to visit her tomorrow."

"I'll go in with Shaley." Ross put a hand on my arm. "Come on, hon."

My insides felt like Jell-O. Somehow I managed to fall into step with Ross. Together we followed Dr. Devlor around the corner and into the examining room.

6

The room was all steel and white, full of medical instruments. Cold. Frightening.

Mom lay on a gurney, covered with a blanket. Her blonde hair was mussed on a pillow, her left arm in a blue cast up to her elbow. She managed a crooked, pain-wracked smile. "Hi, Shaley."

"Mom." I scurried over and pressed a hand to her cheek. My throat choked up. "I'm so sorry."

Her eyes drooped. "It's okay. I'll be okay."

"Hey, Rayne." Ross edged up beside me, putting his hand over Mom's.

Regret stitched across her face. "Ross, I'm so sorry. I've messed everything—"

"Nah." He shook his head. "*You* didn't do anything. But those paparazzi are going to pay." Gently, he squeezed her fingers. "How you feeling?"

"Like a truck hit me."

"Well. Not quite that big."

"Excuse me." A dark-haired nurse touched me on the arm. "We're ready to take your mom to her room now."

"A private one?" Ross gave her a firm look.

She nodded. "Our single-bed rooms are taken, so we're giving her one with two beds but turning it into a private room for as long as she stays."

"Thanks," I said. At least that was something positive. Instead of sitting in a chair all night, I'd have a bed to sleep in. Because no way was I leaving my mom.

The nurse focused on me. "You can come with her if you like."

"Oh. Yeah." I looked around. "I left our purses out there ..."

"I'll get them," Ross said. "And I'll talk to Mick and Wendell. I want them taking turns posted at the door outside her room."

Ross hurried out on his mission.

I stayed close to Mom's gurney as two young orderlies wheeled her into an elevator. "I'm so sorry this happened to you, Miss O'Connor," one of them said as he pushed the button for floor three. He was sandy-haired, with a boyish face. As much as he was trying to act professional, I could tell he felt more than dazzled to be in Rayne O'Connor's presence. "I love your music. I've got all your CDs."

Mom managed a smile. "That's great. Thanks."

Floor three was darkened and quiet, with a metallic, sterile smell. I walked with arms crossed and shoulders drawn in, hating the feel of the place. The two orderlies rolled Mom inside room 321. I looked around at two beds with mustard-yellow spreads, a couple of wooden chairs for visitors. On a rolling, high table pushed against the wall sat a small computer. A swiveling TV was mounted on the wall in the center of the room. Two curved steel rods ran across the ceiling between the beds, housing long blue curtains that could be pulled around for privacy. I swept both curtains all the way back to the wall.

The window overlooked a street lit with lampposts that failed to chase away all the shadows. For a second I stared at the pavement, struck with the thought that the rest of the world was sleeping as if this was some ordinary night.

"Which bed?" the sandy-haired orderly asked.

"Here by the window," I told him. "Okay, Mom? It's farther away from sounds in the hall."

"Okay."

"You got it." They lined up Mom's gurney with her bed.

"All right, ready now?" The second orderly gave her a smile. "We're just going to slide you over."

"Okay." Mom's voice was pinched, as if she knew it would hurt.

He nodded. "One, two, three — go." With one smooth motion, they slid her over. Mom groaned at the movement.

A short, gray-haired nurse came in and introduced herself as Anne. She fussed with Mom's adjustable bed, pushing the button until Mom could sit propped up on pillows. "You won't be able to sleep lying down for awhile, hon," she said. "Those injuries will just hurt too much for you to get up and down."

Mom grunted. "Tell me about it."

I stood back, hands to my mouth, wishing I could take my mother's place.

The orderlies left. Anne put a pitcher of water and a glass by Mom's bedside. She showed me the button for calling a nurse, and how to move Mom's bed up and down.

Ross hustled in, carrying our purses. Mom managed to chuckle at the sight.

"Yeah." Ross thumped them down on a chair in the corner. "Got some strange looks on the way up."

Mom's smile faded. "You need to take care of Shaley."

"No problem."

"I'm staying here, Mom," I said. "I'll be taking care of *you.*"

"No, Shaley, you can't stay here. Go to the hotel and get a decent sleep. You can come back tomorrow."

I looked to Anne and shook my head. "This *is* a private room, right? I can stay if I want."

She tilted her head in a reluctant yes. "Nobody's going to kick you out."

Ross considered me for a moment. "Rayne." He pushed a strand of hair off her forehead. "It'll be safe for Shaley to be here. We'll have Wendell and Mick outside, around the clock. Besides, she wants to help look after you."

Mom's eyelids fluttered. "I just … want …"

Anne gave Mom's arm a sympathetic pat. "The medication's putting her to sleep. It's the best thing for her."

"Yeah." I focused on Mom's bruised forehead.

After Anne left, Ross stayed another ten minutes until Mom was fully asleep. We turned off the lights, except for a small lamp hooked to my bed.

"I'll bring your suitcases in the morning." He headed for the door.

"Ross?"

He turned back. "Yeah?"

"The tour's totally done, isn't it? I mean, no way she can sing before four weeks are over."

He blew out a sigh. "Afraid so."

I looked at the floor.

"See you tomorrow, Shaley."

"Yeah. Good night."

As Ross opened the door, I caught a glimpse of Mick, sitting on a chair in the hall.

The door closed, and suddenly I felt so alone. I looked around the functional, cold-feeling room.

I can't believe this. We're in a hospital.

My eyes landed on a plain white clock on the wall. It was past one o'clock in the morning.

I crossed the room to Mom's bed and gazed down at her. Now that she was asleep, she looked so relaxed, free of pain. If only she could sleep through the whole healing process.

Something inside my body gave way, and my legs went weak. I stumbled to my bed and sank upon it.

In two days' time I'd seen three people killed, been chased by a madman, and stalked by a paparazzo. I'd hardly eaten or slept. And now this accident. No wonder I felt like a wet noodle.

Stretching out on the bed, I tried to remember my life three days ago. When everything had been *normal*. The memories felt distant and grayed. I'd been counting the hours until Brittany could join us on tour —

Brittany.

I needed to call her about Mom. We hadn't talked since before the concert.

Rolling toward one side, I slipped my cell phone out of my back jeans pocket. In that very moment, it went off — Brittany's ring tone.

I punched the button to answer, throwing an anxious look at Mom. She didn't move. I'd have to speak softly. "Hi, Br — "

"Shaleeeey!" Brittany screamed in my ear. She was sobbing. "What's going *on*? I just saw Rayne on TV — being hit by a car!"

"It's on TV? Already?"

What a stupid question. Of course it was on TV. The reporters probably dashed all the way to their stations. Now the whole nation could gawk at the sight of my mom getting hurt.

"Shaley, what — "

"Wait." The meaning of her words slammed into me. "Just what did you see?"

Reporters had been everywhere. I knew they'd filmed Mom lying on the ground. But had one of the TV cameras managed to shoot through all the bodies and film the actual accident — and the seconds leading up to it?

Cat pushing Mom.

If someone got that on camera — we'd have proof.

7

"Hang on, Brittany."

Cell phone clamped to my ear, I yanked the TV remote from a metal roll table beside my bed and punched the power button. The sound sprang on to a loud, blaring commercial.

"Ah!" I threw another frantic look at Mom, praying I hadn't woken her up, my fingers scrambling for *Mute*.

My nerves sizzled. Where *was* the stupid thing?

"Brit, wait a minute." I threw down my phone, took the remote in both hands, and jabbed the TV off. In the jarring silence, I looked for the mute button, my pulse beating double-time. When I found it, I turned the TV back on and immediately pushed the sound off. A car commercial snapped into silence.

I took a deep breath. Glowing light from the TV spilled into the room, onto Mom's still form. She slept on.

I snatched up my phone. "What channel is it on?"

"Any cable news channel, pick one! Shaley! What happened?"

Flicking through channels, I told her. "But did you see everything? Even Cat pushing her?"

"I — I don't know. I was just sitting here, flipping channels, and suddenly there's a reporter talking about Rayne O'Connor — and then this bit of tape — "

"Wait." The hospital TV landed on CNN. A reporter was talking into a microphone, the hotel entrance in the background. I pushed the sound back on and pressed *volume* to turn it way down. "It's on CNN right now."

"Okay, I'll get it." Vaguely, I registered the rustle of her movements over the line.

We fell silent. I leaned forward, gaze glued to the TV. The scene switched to taped footage. Holding my breath, I watched the horrible scene play out. It started choppily, as if the cameraman was running. The picture focused on Mom and Cat. For a moment they disappeared behind the limo as the cameraman ran around behind the car for an unobstructed shot. Then — Cat's crimson face, his camera on the ground. Cat shouting, Mom shouting. Pounding feet approaching as other reporters crowded in. For a moment all I saw was jarring bodies.

"Shaley, no!" Mick's shout sounded on the TV. Still I saw nothing but shirts and arms and heads as the cameraman fought for a clear shot.

This is when Mick shoved me back into the limo.

My right hand clenched. For once I wanted a cameraman to have found his target. "Come on, come on."

The camera jerked and aimed directly toward Cat. In that instant, rage twisted his face — and he rushed Mom.

Brittany gasped.

My limbs went cold. I wanted this on film, but I didn't want to see it. Yet my eyes couldn't tear away.

Heart pounding, I watched my mom stumble ... the car hit. Screams erupted from the crowd. My own figure tore out of the limo toward Mom —

I wrenched my focus from the screen.

For a moment, Brittany and I couldn't speak.

Vengeance sprouted in my chest and grew like some voracious weed. "It's on camera," I said through clenched teeth. "We have the proof *on camera.*"

Cat was going to fry.

Brittany sniffed. "How is she?"

"In a lot of pain. Three fractured ribs and a broken wrist."

"Oh." Empathy tightened Brittany's voice. "What about Cat — where did he go? Did they catch him?"

"He ran. But they will. If they don't, I'll go out and hunt him down myself. And Ross said he's going to sue *Cashing In*."

"I thought you said it's hard to sue those guys because you all are famous."

"This is different. Their photographer caused an *accident*. Plus, because of this, we have to cancel the tour. Can you imagine how much money that's going to cost the band?"

Brittany breathed heavily over the line. "Where are you?"

"In the hospital with Mom. She's sleeping."

"How long does she have to stay?"

I told her.

"Can you come home then?"

"I don't know." A sudden sob rolled up my throat. "I don't know anything anymore. I just want to be *home*. I just want to be with *you*. And Mom to be well. What *is* this, Brittany? What's happening to us? My life has gone totally *insane*."

Brittany's voice cracked. "I wish I was there with you."

"I know. Me too."

We talked until our tears ran out, then talked some more. Weariness pulsed through me, but I couldn't hang up. Not yet. I crept into the bathroom and fetched tissues to wipe my nose. Collapsed again on my bed.

"There's more, Brittany." I looked over toward Mom, making sure she still slept. "Something I haven't told you."

"Like all this isn't *enough*?"

"This is ... I don't know. Almost worse."

I stretched out on my back, staring at the white ceiling. "I told you the cops shot Jerry. Just before he died, he told me something no one else heard."

My fingers clenching the bed covers, I told Brittany Jerry's final words: *Your father sent me.*

"*What?*" Brittany burst. "What does it mean?"

"I don't know."

"Oh. Wow." Brittany exhaled loudly. I could almost hear the wheels in her head turning. "Okay, just ... Let's think about this."

Like a detective, she started firing off questions. It was her logical side coming through, the steely mind that would one day make her a great lawyer. I tried to think straight enough to give her all the details she wanted. My brain was *so* tired.

"Do you think it's true?" Brittany finally asked.

"I don't know."

"But if it is ..."

"I know. If it is, my father sent a killer to us. And somewhere out there, my father's still alive. Maybe he'll try it again."

"Did you tell your mom?"

"No. First, there wasn't time. She had to perform, and then right after that, this happened. I was going to when we got the chance, but I can't now. It would *so* upset her, and she's got enough to deal with."

"The police need to hear this."

"I know. But how can I tell them without telling Mom?"

"Maybe you could tell Ross."

I rubbed a hand over my face. "Yeah, I guess. But that would feel so ... I don't know, like having our privacy invaded. I mean, Mom never talks about my father, even to me."

"You don't know how much Ross knows. Maybe your mom's told him everything."

"No. She wouldn't. She's just too private about it. Besides, Ross is business. This is personal."

We fell silent. My head buzzed with exhaustion. Another few minutes and I wouldn't be able to think at all.

I glanced at the clock. After two a.m.

"Brittany, I don't know if I can stay awake much longer."

"Yeah, me either. We barely got any sleep last night."

"And I don't know how much I'll get tonight. Probably as long as Mom's medication keeps her asleep. When she wakes up, she'll be hurting."

"Poor Rayne."

We both sighed.

"I'll call you in the morning, okay, Brittany?"

"Okay. Good night."

We clicked off.

I turned my head toward Mom — and got a shock. Her eyes were open and troubled, her head turned toward me. Lines crisscrossed her forehead.

"Mom?" I shoved myself into a sitting position. "You're awake already?"

"You know how I am with pain medication." Her voice was weak. "Takes a lot … to knock me out for long."

"But — how long have you … ?"

"Long enough to hear what you didn't want to tell me."

8

He stared at the TV in his cheap motel room, anger churning in his veins.

Just that afternoon he'd stepped out of jail a free man for the first time in eight years. Man, the feeling! Sun on his skin, fresh air. He could go where he wanted, eat what he wanted. Sleep in a real bed.

Sizzling with anticipation, he caught a bus for the short trip into Phoenix.

At midnight he sank down on the edge of the bed, shoes off, tired to the bone. He flipped on the TV — and saw Rayne O'Connor screaming at a photographer.

Three times, the cable news channel played footage of the scene.

"Rayne O'Connor is now in Denver's St. Joseph's Hospital, reportedly with multiple cracked ribs," a perky blonde news anchor said. "She is expected to have a full, though long, recovery. This on the very same night that Rayne's sixteen-year-old daughter, Shaley, was taken hostage by Jerry Brand, a man hired to drive one of the rock band's buses. Brand is the alleged killer of two men on tour — Tom Hutchens, hair stylist and makeup artist, and bodyguard Bruce Stolz. Police fatally shot Brand during the rescue of Shaley O'Connor ..."

His mouth had fallen open. His fingers clenched the TV remote.

Now here he sat, jaw hardened to granite, a buzz in his head.

The police had to be lying.

But the last few times he'd tried to call Jerry to check in, Jerry hadn't answered his cell phone. Had the man been avoiding him on purpose?

Now Jerry was dead.

"... no official word yet on the Rayne tour, which is scheduled to continue for another month." The reporter's voice pierced his consciousness. "But given the popular singer's injuries, it is expected to be cancelled. And now to —"

He switched the channel, seeking other cable news stations. Once again, Rayne's face filled the screen.

Eyes narrowed, he listened to every word of the report. When it ended he found a third station running the story. And a fourth.

He flipped channel after channel until he saw no more. He punched off the TV.

The rage simmered in his stomach, building to a full boil. He shoved off the bed and strode around the small room, fingers pressed to his temples.

What had Jerry done? Now there'd be more cops than ever around Rayne and Shaley O'Connor.

That afternoon he'd walked out of jail to the inheritance left by his grandmother. The sale of her small Phoenix home had netted Franklin a profit around $50,000. He'd only withdrawn a few hundred to stay in this cheap place for one night. He had plans for the rest of the money.

After the bank he'd gone to the DMV to renew his expired driver's license.

He flung himself on the bed and stared at the ceiling. He'd waited years to get to Rayne and Shaley O'Connor. Now, thanks to Jerry, it would be harder than ever. But he'd do it.

Denver. That's where he'd be headed tomorrow. St. Joseph's Hospital in Denver.

9

stared at Mom, my brain going numb. She'd *heard* my conversation with Brittany? My throat convulsed. "Mom—"

"It's okay. I had to know."

I pushed to my feet and crossed to her side. "But—"

"You really expected to deal with this alone, Shaley?"

"No. But I just ... I would have told you later."

"The detective asked you what Jerry had whispered to you just before he died. You told him, 'Nothing important.'"

"I couldn't say the real words then." I slipped a hand over my eyes. How to explain what I'd felt at that moment? For years I'd begged for answers about my dad, and there I was, supposed to blurt out terrible words about him to some detective I'd never seen before in my life? "I knew it would upset you and ... I don't know, the words just balled up inside me. I couldn't talk about it then."

Mom's eyes clouded. I bit my lip, wishing she'd say something—*anything*. If she hadn't been doped up on pain medication, she wouldn't be taking this so quietly. "So ... do you think Jerry was telling the truth?" I asked.

Mom stared beyond me, brow knitting, as if she peered into a bitter past. "Why would he say something like that if he didn't know your father?"

"I don't know."

"A person's last words are important. With his last dying breath, he chose to say that to you."

I ran a finger along the bed cover, feeling its fine ridges. Mom was saying what my gut had been telling me. I couldn't even figure how I felt about that. Part of me wanted Jerry's words to be a lie. How could I cling to the hope of any goodness in my father if he'd sent Jerry to our tour? But if it was true, at least my father was out there somewhere, and he *knew* I was his daughter. Mom had always claimed he didn't. Maybe there was a good explanation for what he'd done. Maybe he didn't know Jerry was so messed up in the head ...

Mom's eyes slipped shut.

I touched her shoulder. "Are you in pain?"

"Not as long as I don't move." She tried to smile. She focused on me, her eyes glazed. "Tomorrow you have to call the detective who interviewed you after Jerry was shot and tell him this."

Detective Myner, the short, gray-haired man with the hard-worn face. Could that really have been just eight hours ago?

My vision blurred. "You always told me my dad doesn't know about me."

"I ... didn't think he did."

"Do you think he'd want to hurt us?"

All these years of begging her to tell me about my father. Had she kept quiet because she knew he hated her? That he was nothing but a lowdown, murderous criminal?

"Shaley. You *will* call Detective Myner tomorrow."

So much for an answer. My eyes blinked hard, trying to chase the tears away, but they spilled onto my cheeks. I nodded. "Okay."

Mom swallowed. "Can you get me a drink?"

"Sure." I poured some water from her pitcher into a glass. "Here's a straw." I picked it off the tray and inserted it into the glass. Held it to her lips.

Mom took three long drinks, then closed her eyes. I put the glass back on the tray and gazed at her.

Just yesterday we'd fought about my father. The age-old resentment in me could so easily erupt. I *deserved* to hear some answers. Who was my dad? Where did he go? Why had I never seen him? But

Mom would never tell me. I only knew one detail. While they were dating he'd often give her a single white rose wrapped in green cellophane and tied with a red ribbon. To this day that symbol seemed sacred to her, although she'd never told me the full story behind it.

Mom's eyes opened. We gazed at each other, silent communication flowing between us. If she wasn't in a hospital bed, all banged up, we'd probably be fighting over this right now. I'd be accusing her of almost getting us killed through hanging on to her secrets. She'd be stubbornly refusing to talk ...

For the first time it occurred to me that maybe some good could come out of this terrible accident.

"Mom." I rubbed her shoulder. "Answer me."

Her mouth turned downward. "The person I loved would never want to hurt us. But that person went away long ago. If he sent Jerry to us, he only meant us harm."

I pulled my arms across my chest, bitterness edging my voice. "You need to tell me about him. No excuses anymore. You and I are stuck here anyway, so we might as well talk."

Mom made a sound in her throat. The glaze of pain in her eyes changed to grief. "I just ... some things are hard to ... But you're right. You deserve to know."

All I could do was stare. Had I really heard that? After all my years of wanting to know, she was finally going to tell me?

Mom looked past me, into the distance. "Where to start? There's so much ..."

I hurried to the corner of the room and dragged over one of the wooden chairs. Sat down by her bed. My heart picked up speed. This was really happening. I couldn't believe it.

"Start at the beginning."

PART 2
Rayne 1991

10

He was the quiet guy who sat in front of me in French class, and was one year ahead of me in school. He didn't talk much and kept to himself.

Everything about him fascinated me.

It was October, the second month of my sophomore year. Our French teacher was horrible. Mrs. Wright would give us stupid little conversations to memorize and recite to each other. Whenever we had to do that, Gary Donovon would turn around to be my partner.

He had sandy-colored hair and large, almost translucent gray eyes. Long eyelashes. And a way of moving his mouth that was so expressive. He'd firm his lips, pulling them in at the corners whenever he forgot one of his French lines. If he thought something was funny, one corner of his mouth would turn up in this quirky smile. Gary had long fingers, like a pianist's. He was tall and muscled, but graceful, almost loping in his walk. In the crowded hallways, while everyone else jabbered and called out to friends, he'd walk by himself, head slightly tilted to one side, focused straight ahead. Like a rock in the middle of a stream, water flowing around it.

The guy was totally intriguing. And he didn't even know it.

"Hi, Veronique," Gary said to me that Thursday as he turned around in his seat.

"Hi, Simon."

Each of us had a French name we had to use in class. In the French pronunciation, Gary's name — Simon — sounded like SeeMOH.

Gary/Simon met my eyes for a split second, then looked away. Why did he always do that? Every other guy tended to stare me up and down. The popular, cocky ones all tried to impress me. The unpopular ones treated me like some princess on a pedestal. I didn't particularly care for any of that.

But Gary was different. He was good-looking, but not at all arrogant about it. Quiet, but not self-effacing. He didn't even seem to want many friends, as if his aloneness contented him.

How could anyone be content without tons of friends?

I knew lots of people at our large high school, plus many more at surrounding schools. My freshman yearbook was so marked up with written notes, you could hardly see half the pictures. While Gary obviously would hate the limelight, I sought it, singing to anybody who'd listen. In fact, one day I *knew* I was going to be lead singer in a band.

Nothing about us was the same. None of my friends would ever think of putting the two of us together.

So why did Gary Donovon pull at me so much?

"Hey, Simon." I tapped my desk with a long red fingernail. My voice held a tinge of amusement. "I'm over here."

His gray eyes scanned back to me.

I held his gaze, a little smile on my face. "You know the conversation?"

He shrugged. "Yeah."

All around us buzzed fifteen versions of our French assignment for the day. Our teacher sat at her desk, reading a magazine. "Okay. You take the first line."

Gary focused on my hands. "Aimes-tu les fleurs?" *Do you like flowers?*

"Oui, très bien." *Yes, I like them very much.*

"Lequel est-ce que tu aimes le mieux?" *Which is your favorite?*

"La rose blanche." *A white rose.*

Gary shifted in his chair. "Vraiment? Pourquoi?" *Really? Why?*

The last line of Mrs. Wright's conversation was totally lame.

"Les roses blanches sont purs et frais. Je veux les toucher." *White roses look pure and fresh. They make me want to touch them.*

Gary's gaze rose again to my face. Long seconds passed as he looked at me, his lips pressing together. For the first time I noticed darker gray flecks around the outside of his irises.

Strange. It almost felt like he wanted to tell me something…

I waited.

His gaze fell away.

A sigh puffed from my lips. "Forget the last line?"

His head pulled back. "No. I just …" He cleared his throat, then rattled off the sentence. "Ah, j'ai pensé que tu préférais les roses rouges." *Oh. I thought you'd like red ones better.*

I nodded. "Well. Very good. I give you an A."

One half of his mouth curved. He still wouldn't look at me. "You get an A too."

And with that, he turned around and faced the front.

I stared at the back of his head. *What was it with this guy?* Everybody else was still talking, and the teacher would read that magazine of hers for another good ten minutes.

An even bigger question filled my thoughts. Why was I afraid to ask him why he cut our conversation short — again? With any other guy I'd push it in a flirty way — "Hey, why won't you talk? Something wrong with me?"

Instead I sat back, arms folded, focusing on his neck just above the collar line of his blue shirt. The bottom of his hair looked a little ragged, like it needed trimming.

He was going to tell me something. I felt it.

For two months I would wonder what it was.

11

One day in early December I walked into French class and saw the school principal standing near Mrs. Wright's desk. I dropped my pink three-ring binder on my desk and plopped down. What was up?

As soon as the bell rang, the principal announced that Mrs. Wright had just gone home sick, and there was no one to take her place.

"You all need to stay in this room, understand? I don't want to find anyone walking the halls. And keep the noise down."

With that, he left — and we had a free hour.

The room immediately hummed with conversation. In front of me, Gary sat unmoving, long legs stretched out, head tilted. From what I could tell, he was staring at the floor.

What on earth does he think about so much?

"Hey, Rayne," Cindy called from two rows over.

I looked around. She was already forming a circle of desks with Crystal and Nikki. Normally I'd have been right there with them. But for over three months now, good-looking, quiet Gary Donovon had remained a puzzle to me. Here was my chance to figure him out.

I tapped him on the shoulder.

He turned around and looked at me, eyebrows raised. His face looked strained.

All the words that usually flowed off my tongue dried up. I gave him a tentative smile. "Hi, Gary."

"Hi." He smiled back.

"You look tired."

He pulled in a deep breath. "Didn't sleep much last night. My grandma was sick."

"Your grandma?"

"Yeah. I live with her."

"Oh." Usually it was the other way around. "You mean she moved into your parents' house?"

Gary gave me a long look. His expression whisked me back to that morning in October, when I'd sensed something behind his gray eyes. "No. I live with *her*. My parents are dead."

My eyes widened. "Oh, wow. I'm so sorry."

He looked away, his lips pressed. "It's okay. They were in a car accident when I was six. Grandma Helen raised me."

I rubbed a finger across the bottom of my binder. What would that be like, being raised by someone so much older? And losing *both* your parents?

"I live with my mom," I told him. "My parents divorced when I was three."

His chin raised in a slight nod. "You ever see your father?"

I focused on a smudge in the upper corner of my notebook. Rubbed at it with my thumb. "Not anymore. I don't even try to." My voice tinged with a bitterness I'd typically hold back. Only a few close friends knew my feelings about my father. "He only lives about an hour away. When I was a kid he used to call and say, 'I'll come see you, and we'll do this or that' — all sorts of fun stuff. I'd count the days, all excited, and that morning be bouncing around, waiting for him. And then he wouldn't show."

Gary's eyes held mine. I felt something connect between us.

He curled his left hand around the back of his desk. "That's hard."

"Yeah."

We fell silent for a moment. Gary's gaze dropped to the floor.

I could hear Nikki jabbering away, telling some story. Crystal was laughing in that high-pitched giggle of hers.

I reached out and laid my fingers on the back of Gary's hand. His eyes snapped back to mine, surprised.

I eased away, resting my hand on my desk, not far from his. "What's wrong with your grandmother?"

"She's had heart trouble for a long time. Now she has the flu, and it just wears her out. Twice in the night she needed water and couldn't get out of bed, so she called for me. I worry about her, you know? I'm all she's got to take care of her."

I could picture it. Gary, bringing water to his grandmother, hanging around to make sure she was okay. No wonder I never saw him out partying or at football games. He had responsibilities at home.

All the guys I'd dated were so into their friends and having a good time. Come to think of it, so was I. Suddenly all that seemed shallow.

"Rayne!" Crystal called.

I turned and gave my three friends a grin.

Nikki gestured emphatically. "Come *over* here!"

"Go ahead," Gary said. "It's okay."

Later, I mouthed to my friends. I rotated toward Gary. "I can see them anytime. I'd rather talk to you."

His jaw worked back and forth as he looked at me. A tiny smile curved one side of his mouth. "That so."

It was more of a statement than a question. I held his gaze, feeling a little tingle inside. Was Gary Donovon *flirting* with me?

"You ever go out at night?" I blurted.

He shrugged. "When I can. I work a lot of hours a week, helping this guy out with his moving company."

Lifting furniture. So that's where his muscles came from.

"I never see you at football games or anything."

There came that little smile again. "Didn't know you were looking for me."

Okay, he *was* flirting. This I could handle. "Maybe I just notice things around me."

"You'd have to look through a lot of people."

"What's that mean?"

"You're usually surrounded by lots of friends. Girls *and* guys."

I leaned forward, fixed him with a knowing smile of my own. "Sounds like you've been looking for me too."

"Maybe I just notice things around me." Gary looked straight into my eyes. As if daring me on.

Whoa. There was way more to this guy than I thought. I'd expected him to be all shy and everything. A flush crept into my cheeks. Before I could stop myself, my gaze fell to my binder.

Well, great. Now what? And — wouldn't you know it — Gary was back to saying nothing. He just sat there watching me, waiting for me to find my tongue.

Fine then.

I raised my eyes to his. "You know Nikki over there?"

Gary glanced at her. "Yeah."

"She's having a party at her house this Saturday night. Want to go with me?"

Gary didn't even blink. "I thought the guy was supposed to ask the girl out."

"I'm not asking you out. It's just a party."

"Could have fooled me."

He said it teasingly enough, but it still ticked me off. I leaned back and shrugged. "Never mind then."

"I didn't say I didn't want to go."

My jaw firmed. "Could have fooled me."

Both sides of his mouth curved. Definitely the biggest smile I'd ever seen on his face. My irritation slid away.

He bounced a fist against the back of his chair. "Nikki won't mind?"

"No. She'll be glad you came."

Listen to us now. Suddenly so polite. I felt that old distance between us edge back, and I didn't want it.

"Gary."

"Huh?"

"You remember a couple months ago, when our French conversation was about white roses?"

A look came into his eyes. "Yeah."

Something about his expression almost made me lose my nerve. I didn't want to ask the question and be refused an answer. "Your last line. You wanted to say something else. What was it?"

He pressed his lips and looked away. Ran a finger along his jaw. "What's your address?"

I gave him a look. "You mean you're not going to tell me?"

"What's your address?"

I sighed and told him. He wrote it down.

"What time should I pick you up for the party?"

"I don't know." My voice sounded sullen. I was still fixed on the unanswered question. "Seven, I guess."

He nodded. "I'll be there."

I heard finality in his voice, like the conversation was over. He started to turn around.

I caught his hand. "Why won't you tell me?"

His gray eyes looked deeply into mine, as if trying to figure out if he could trust me. "Tell you what — I will. On Saturday." He smiled. "Thanks for asking me."

"Sure."

He turned to face the front. Just like that.

I folded my arms, staring at the back of his head. Wondering what on earth had just happened.

The three days before the party passed so slowly. Mrs. Wright was out sick for all that week, and her sub didn't make us do the French conversations. Gary and I barely talked.

Finally Saturday arrived. That afternoon the doorbell rang. It was a delivery from a florist. A long white box with an envelope addressed to me.

Somehow, I knew. *Gary*.

I hurried to my bedroom and shut the door. Sat down on my bed. Slowly, holding my breath, I lifted the box's cover.

Inside was an absolutely beautiful white rose, not yet fully opened. It was long-stemmed, wrapped in green cellophane, and tied with a red ribbon.

For some time I held the delicate flower to my nose, breathing in its sweet scent.

Carefully, I laid the rose down and reached for the envelope. Inside was a folded card. Gary had written our French conversation.

> *Do you like flowers?*
> *Yes, I like them very much.*
> *Which is your favorite?*
> *A white rose.*
> *Really? Why?*
> *White roses look pure and fresh. They make me*
>   *want to touch them.*

And the last line — the words he'd wanted to say two months ago.

> *You are a white rose to me.*

PART 3

Monday 2009

12

I awoke to the sound of voices.

Blinking hard to clear my vision, I pushed up in the hospital bed and glanced at the clock. It was after eight.

A brown-haired nurse was dropping two pills into Mom's palm and holding out a glass of water. Mom downed the medication with one gulp. Her eyes were half-closed, her expression stretched with pain.

"All right, let's get you up to the bathroom." The nurse folded Mom's bedcovers down to her feet.

Apprehension curled around my shoulders. I slid out of bed, the clothes I'd slept in feeling wrinkled and sweaty. "Mom, you okay?"

The nurse turned toward me. She had a long face and big eyes, a placid smile. Her name tag read *Helen Trevor.* "She's fine. Just giving her more pain meds."

"Hey, Shaley." Mom's voice hitched. "Glad to ... see you ... got some sleep."

I walked around the foot of the bed and to Mom's other side. Her heavy stage mascara was smudged under her eyes, the foundation makeup and blush looking cakey. With a pang I realized she'd never even had the chance to wash her face.

Mom reached for me with her casted arm, and our fingers brushed.

Gary Donovon. My father's name is Gary Donovon.

I rubbed my thumb over hers. "Thanks for our talk last night."

She nodded.

Mom had talked until around three in the morning, when she finally dozed off. I drank in every word, imagining the sound of my father's voice, his face. Picturing the scene as Mom opened the card with the white rose. "More," I wanted to beg when she had to stop, "tell me more!" But she needed to sleep.

My father's name had echoed in my mind as I climbed into bed.

Now, looking into Mom's eyes, I wondered — what happened? How did they start officially dating? And what made him leave in the end — *forever*?

"Okay, Rayne, let's get this done now." The nurse was all business.

Mom grimaced. "Can't wait."

Helen made little tsking noises. "I know those ribs are really sore, so let's get you sitting up as far as we can first." She hit a button, and the top of the bed rose to its highest position.

"Can I help?" I asked.

"Yes. Put your arms behind your mom's back and ease her up a full ninety degrees. Then I'll rotate her legs toward the floor."

I hesitated. "Okay, Mom?"

She gave me a little nod, trying to smile.

I slipped my arms between her back and the mattress. Mom made a grinding sound in her throat. I threw a frantic look at the nurse — *I'm hurting her!*

"It's all right," she said. "Just nice and slow."

Holding my breath, I eased Mom upright. Her eyes squeezed shut.

"Okay now, hang on to her and I'll move those feet around." The nurse reached for Mom's legs and moved them across the bed until her feet were just off the mattress. Mom hissed air through her teeth. "This is where it gets a little tougher, Rayne, because you're going to have to use your own good arm and muscles to scoot forward and get up."

With every movement Mom clenched her jaw harder. By the

time she stood on shaky feet, supported by Helen, my own teeth ached.

"All right now, walk slow and easy." Helen held on to Mom's right arm.

Mom's baby steps to the bathroom were slow and painstaking. I watched her, throat tight, the old anger at paparazzi popping inside me like oil in a hot skillet.

Where was Cat this morning? Caught, I hope.

As Mom and the nurse disappeared into the bathroom and closed the door, I switched on the TV. The first cable news channel was talking about stocks. I flipped to the second — and saw the footage of Cat and Mom arguing. My fingers dug into the remote. I could *not* see that accident one more time. Biting my lip, I focused on my unmade bed, counting the seconds until it ended.

The sound of my own taped screaming wrenched my eyes back to the screen. I saw myself jump from the limo and rush toward Mom …

Last night's anguish and disbelief pelted me all over again. I could almost hear the crowd around me, feel the pavement hard beneath my feet —

The picture switched to a reporter standing outside the hotel in daylight. "This morning the police are still looking for the *Cashing In* photographer, Len Torret …"

I clenched my teeth. Cat was still out there. Meanwhile my Mom was here in a hospital, every move hurting her. It wasn't right. It wasn't *fair*.

The TV remote felt moist in my palm. I threw it onto my bed and stalked to the window, staring out into the back street behind the hospital. Frustration boiled inside me. I didn't want to be trapped inside this stale and sterile room. For once I wished for a badge and a gun. I'd hunt down Cat myself.

My fingers pressed into the narrow ledge beneath the window. Gazing fitfully at the street below, I saw a car back up toward the curb in a parallel park. Across the road a mother pushed a stroller on the sidewalk. Some distance behind her walked a man with a large backpack.

Wait.

I leaned closer to the window, squinting at the man. He was too far away for me to see his face clearly, although I could tell he was completely bald. He was dressed in jeans and a black T-shirt. His arms and legs looked gangly. And the way he moved — he didn't walk. He slunk.

At that moment, almost as if he felt me, his head turned and tilted up toward my window. I jerked back.

Cat.

For a second I could hardly believe it. He was here. Right *here.* But of course he would be. He was Cat. He never gave up.

I ran for my cell phone. Snatching it up, I yanked Officer Hanston's card from my front jeans pocket. My finger shook as I punched in his number.

"Officer Hanston."

"Hi. It's Shaley O'Connor." The words spilled out of me. "That photographer who pushed my mom is outside the hospital! I just saw him out my window."

"Okay, slow down. Tell me exactly what you saw."

I hurried back to the window, taking care not to stand too close. My neck strained toward the street below. "I can't see him any-more." I told the officer what Cat was wearing and that he'd shaved his head. "And he's carrying a big backpack. I bet his camera's in there."

"All right. I'll send some officers over to have a look."

"Please let me know if they find him."

"I will. Thanks."

I ended the call and pressed my forehead against the glass, look-ing up and down the street. No sign of Cat.

It wasn't hard to guess what he was trying to do. While all the other reporters and photographers hung around the main entrance, hoping to hear some news about Rayne O'Connor, Cat would want the big prize — a picture of Mom in her hospital room. His trashy tabloid would probably pay a hundred thousand dollars or more for it. Cat would do anything for that kind of money.

"Well, you're not going to get it," I declared aloud. I stomped toward the door and yanked it open. If Cat was somewhere in this hospital, I was going to find him.

13

Wendell looked around as I shot through the door. "Shaley, where are you going?"

I didn't slow. "Just want to walk around for awhile."

"Don't do that."

"It won't hurt anything."

He rose and caught my arm. "Stop."

I halted and glared up at him. His hair was back to its usual perfect form, gelled up straight. Looked like he'd gotten some sleep. Memories of last evening flooded my head. Just a little over twelve hours ago this guy had saved my life.

My tone softened. "Wendell, I'm not leaving the hospital, okay?"

"You shouldn't be leaving this room."

"I've got to *go*!"

"Why?"

"Cat's here. I'm going to find him."

His head pulled back. "No you're not."

"If anybody can draw him out, *I* can."

He reached for the cell phone clipped to his waist. "I'll call the police — "

"I already did!" I pulled my arm from his grasp and turned to head down the hall.

"Shaley, stop." He grabbed my shoulders.

"Let me go, Wendell!"

"No."

I struggled to pull away, but he held firm. Tears clawed my eyes.

Why did everybody think I was so helpless? Mom deserved justice. I *couldn't* let Cat get away. My arms rose and before I knew it, I was pummeling Wendell in the chest. Frustration and anger balled up inside me, driving my punches harder. Sobs tumbled up my throat. "Let me go, Wendell!"

"Stop, Shaley, shhhh, stop." He wrapped his muscular arms around me and pulled me in tight until I couldn't move. I tried to break free, but no way; he was too strong.

Sudden exhaustion filled me, sweeping away the anger. I went limp against him and cried.

One of his hands came up to pat the back of my head. "Yeah, I know, kid. I know. It's okay."

My cell phone went off. I choked down my tears. "That might be the police."

Wendell released his grip. I backed up and pulled my phone out of my pocket, checking the ID through blurry eyes. It was Ross.

I wiped my face and took a shaky breath before answering. "Hi, Ross."

"Hi. You okay?"

I met Wendell's eyes. He gave me a look, warning me not to try running down the hall again. "Yeah. I'm fine. Just tired."

He grunted. "How's Rayne?"

"In a lot of pain. But she's up and with a nurse in the bathroom. You coming over? I need my clothes, and Mom needs hers. And I need food."

"Okay, okay. I'll see what I can do."

Ross clicked off the line. I lowered my phone and aimed an embarrassed look at Wendell. "I'm sorry."

He shrugged. "Don't worry about it."

I brushed hair out of my face. "I just want to catch Cat so bad after what he did ..."

"I know."

Mom's hospital door opened and the nurse stuck her head out. "Oh, there you are. Your mom was worried about you."

"I'm coming."

The nurse disappeared, leaving the door half open. I stepped toward it. "Wendell, thanks again for all you did last night. And I'm really sorry."

"Hey, forget it. We're all a little uptight right now."

No kidding.

I pushed the door open and went inside.

Mom was back in bed. Her foundation and blush had been washed away, but the eye shadow and mascara remained. It would take her bottled remover to get that heavy stuff off.

As the nurse was taking Mom's blood pressure and temperature, breakfast arrived. Scrambled eggs and bacon, toast, orange juice, and coffee. I fussed with the wheeled tray, bringing it up close to Mom, taking the paper lid off the glass of juice. Inside, I still felt so agitated. Where was Cat? Had the police found him?

"All right." The nurse looked up from the computer, where she'd entered Mom's data. "All set. Just push the button if you need anything."

"Thanks," Mom said.

Helen slipped from the room.

Mom picked up her fork and eyed her breakfast. "I can't believe I'm about to eat eggs and bacon."

"Do it, Mom, you need it."

Something in my tone made her look at me closer. "What's wrong?"

"Cat's around here. I saw him out the window."

Mom put down the fork. I told her what I'd seen and that I'd talked to Officer Hanston. I left out the part about trying to run down the hall and go after Cat myself.

"They'll get him," I said. I had to believe that. "They should be calling me soon." I gestured toward the tray. "Eat."

Mom managed to eat half her breakfast while I paced. *Where was Cat?*

The door opened and a white-coated doctor stepped inside. He was tall and narrow-shouldered, with a round, almost boyish face.

"Knock, knock." He strode across the room to Mom's bed. "I'm Doctor Gedding. How are you doing this morning?"

Mom pushed the tray away. "Okay."

He made an empathetic sound. "I'm sure you're plenty sore. Let me just take a look at that wrapping around your ribs."

"You done with this, Mom?" I pointed to her tray and she nodded. "I'll take it outside."

Wendell sat on his chair, legs spread, arms folded. Staring at the wall. He looked up at the sound of my footsteps. "Hey again."

"Hey." I glanced around. "Am I supposed to leave this on the floor for pick up, like at a hotel?"

"Don't think so. A nurse should come get it."

"Maybe the doctor will take it."

"Doctors don't remove trays. That's beneath them."

Everything in this hospital was frustrating me. "Oh, well excuse me." I set the tray firmly on the opposite side of the door. "There. They don't like it, they can take it away."

The doctor appeared behind me. I stepped from his path. "Everything okay?" I asked.

"As well as can be expected." He patted his coat pocket. His gaze fell to the tray on the floor, then bounced away. "I'll be back to check on her tonight." His shoes squeaked as he hurried down the hall.

Wendell and I exchanged a knowing look.

Back in the room, I hurried over to Mom. "You okay?"

She nodded.

"He hurt you?"

"Everything hurts me."

I stared at the wooden chair, sudden rage shooting through me. For a crazy minute I wanted to yank up the chair and hurl it through the window. This wasn't *right*, having to stay here, Mom being in so much pain.

"Shaley." Mom tugged on my shirt. "Chill. They'll get Cat."

My eyes burned. "I hate this for you."

"I know."

Mom gestured toward the chair. "Sit down. I'll tell you about going to the party with Gary."

Hope glimmered inside me. If I couldn't fix the present, at least I could learn more about the past. "Sure you're up to it?"

"Yeah."

I sat. Half of my mind still fixed on Cat, imagining him slinking the halls. But then Mom gazed beyond me, a wistful expression settling on her face as if she peered into a time she wished had never gone. I felt myself being pulled back into the past I so longed to know.

"I remember pacing my room that December night," Mom began. "Waiting for Gary to pick me up. Thinking the time would never come ..."

PART 4

Rayne 1991

14

Finally — the sound of a car outside. Gary Donovon had arrived.

I edged back my bedroom curtain to see a black truck pull up to the curb outside our house. The door opened and Gary got out. He was wearing beige pants and a tucked-in long-sleeve blue shirt. I'd only seen him in jeans at school.

My breath hitched. He looked so *good*.

Gary headed up the sidewalk with that confident-yet-unassuming walk of his. I dropped the curtain. Didn't want him to catch me watching.

My heart beat a little too hard as I crossed my room. On my dresser in a small, clear vase sat the white rose. I'd used the red ribbon to tie the cellophane like a skirt around the vase. I grinned at the flower as I passed.

This guy was too much.

The doorbell rang.

"Ra-aayne!" my mom called.

"Coming!"

I couldn't remember when I'd been so excited about a date. (Even if I'd told Gary it wasn't a real one.) I'd gone out with lots of guys, and never had any trouble getting their attention. But Gary was ... different.

As I entered the short front hallway, I glanced down at my-self — in tight jeans and a pink, silky shirt. I'd changed outfits five times. *Hope he likes it.*

I opened the door and stood back. "Hey."

"Hey yourself." His eyes grazed down my body and back to my face. "You look beautiful."

How could I not smile at that? "Thanks. Come on in."

Gary stepped inside. I closed the door.

How different it felt, standing next to him. I was used to facing him across a desk. He was a good six inches taller than me. His height made me feel good. Feminine.

I nudged his arm. "Come on, I'll introduce you to my mom."

"Okay."

Mom was lounging on the couch in old jeans and a faded sweat-shirt, no makeup. Worn out from working in her backyard garden all day. She didn't bother to stand as I made the introductions.

"Nice to meet you." Gary held out his hand, and she shook it.

"Likewise." She gave him her *I'm-the-big-bad-mom* frown. "You gonna take care of my daughter?"

"Absolutely."

"She's the only one I got, you know."

Gary threw me a glance. "I'd say you got the best."

Mom drew back her head. "Oh, listen to him, Rayne. Flattery and all."

"No, ma'am. Not flattery. Just fact."

The way he said it — not cocky, like some fast-talking salesman. Just quiet and firm.

Approval gleamed in Mom's eyes. She turned to me. "Twelve o'clock. Not a minute late."

"I know, I know."

Gary and I whisked out the door.

Parties at Nikki's house were always fun. She had a large rec room basement that we could take over while her parents stayed on the main floor. We'd laugh and eat and play CDs, and laugh some more. We had a regular group of friends who always came — about ten girls and their dates. But to me that party with Gary was like none other. All through the evening I felt so *aware* of him, even if we weren't at each other's side every minute. As he talked to other people, when he went to the table for food, as he moved around the room, vibrations seemed to link us. I knew he felt it too.

And he got along easily with everyone. Wasn't quiet, didn't seem shy. All my friends liked him. So why did he keep to himself so much at school?

"You have fun?" I asked as we walked to his car just before midnight. Christmas lights shone from houses up and down the street. The air had turned chilly. I shivered.

"Cold?" He put his arm around my shoulders. It felt good. Right.

"Thanks."

How could this guy have sat in front of me in French class all semester and never shown a bit of interest? And how could he get along so well with everybody at a party but seem so reserved at school?

He opened the passenger door of the truck for me, then walked around the front and got in. The engine roared to life. I watched him out the corner of my eye as he put the truck in gear and started down the street.

"Gary?"

"Yeah?"

"Why did you come with me tonight?"

"Because I wanted to."

"Why did you want to?"

He pressed his lips, his right palm sliding up and down on the steering wheel.

"I mean, all semester you've talked to me only when we had to do one of those stupid French conversations."

"That's the only time you talked to me too. Seemed to me you were pretty busy with all your friends."

My mouth opened to deny it, then shut. It occurred to me, even with the tons of people I knew, how small my world was. Because I only saw what I was used to seeing.

"I'm sorry."

He shrugged. "It's nothing to be sorry about. You're just popular, that's all."

I rubbed the side seam of my jeans. "I've wanted to talk to you for months. You just didn't seem interested."

One side of his mouth curved. He shot me a glance. "I was plenty interested."

"Then why didn't you ... *do* something?"

We stopped at a red light. He inhaled a long breath — and that's when I knew. I could see it written all over his face — the hesitation. He had something to hide.

"Guess I've just got too much going on in my own life. Like I told you, I work a lot, plus I keep an eye out for my grandmother. She doesn't ... we don't live in the best area. I want to make sure she's safe."

Why didn't he think she was safe? What had happened? Questions crowded my tongue, but I bit them back. I didn't want to come across like some Spanish inquisition.

The light turned green. Gary surged the truck forward.

I touched his arm. "Well, I'm glad you came with me tonight."

He threw me a smile. "Me too."

For the rest of the way home, I changed the subject, chatting away about this and that person at the party, making small talk. But I could tell Gary knew what I was doing. Beneath the light conversation ran a darker current — his secrets and my determination to find out what they were.

At my house he walked me to the door. I leaned against it, looked up into his face. "You going to talk to me in French class now?" I said it half-teasingly, but the undercurrent still ran.

He gave me that lopsided smile of his. "Yeah."

"Well. That's something then."

Gary held my eyes, his expression turning serious. I felt a tingle at the back of my neck. He placed a palm against the door, leaned down — and kissed me. His lips were warm and soft. Incredible. A deep longing reached from his soul to mine, a longing that went way beyond physical touch. As if he wanted to tell me things about himself ... but couldn't.

The kiss wasn't long, yet in a way it seemed forever. When Gary pulled back, I knew we would be together for a long time. Whatever he was hiding, it didn't matter. We could work our way through it.

How wrong I would turn out to be.

PART 5
Monday 2009

15

The day had come.

Before checking out of his hotel room, he picked up the phone to make a plane reservation to Denver.

"Operator. What listing please?"

"United Airlines."

"Thank you." The line clicked over to the recorded number. He pulled the hotel pen and notepad forward on the nightstand and wrote down the digits. Firmly, he punched them in.

Put on hold for an agent, he sat on the bed and waited, tapping one hand against his knee.

He needed a plan when he got to Denver. Rayne had to have all kinds of protection around her now. How was he going to get to her?

"United Airlines, this is Sarah. How can I help you?"

He booked a flight leaving at 3:45, arriving in Denver at 5:30. He'd pay for the ticket in cash when he arrived at the airport.

He hung up and checked the digital radio clock. Just past nine. He had things to do before catching the flight. Buy clothes. Get to the bank for more cash. And he needed a cell phone.

Quickly, he stuffed his meager possessions into the paper bag he'd carried out of prison. He stepped from his second floor room to the oven-like heat of a Phoenix June morning and hurried down the long outside corridor to the stairs.

On the street he walked three blocks before spotting a cab to flag down. In the back seat he closed his eyes, remembering prison.

The noises, the smells. The danger. Never knew who'd shank you in the back.

He'd die before he went back there.

The cab slowed. He opened his eyes and saw the bank. Snatching up his paper bag, he slid from the car and paid the cabbie.

Inside the bank, he waited for help at one of the customer service desks. An attractive thirtyish woman with blonde hair beckoned for him to take the seat across from her. He stared at her, thinking of Rayne.

"How can I help you, sir?"

"I need an ATM card."

"All right. Do you have the number for your account?"

"Can you just look it up for me?"

"Sure. I need to see some ID."

He pulled a worn wallet from his back jeans pocket and took out his driver's license. "Here you go." He slid the white piece of paper in front of her.

She smiled, reading his name on the license. "Franklin Borden."

"Yeah." He smiled back. "That's me."

16

Two brisk knocks sounded on Mom's hospital room door. I turned around in my chair near her bed. "Yeah?"

The door opened part way and Ross stuck his head inside. "The cavalry's here. With food."

Disappointment carved through me. Mom's story had so transported me, I almost forgot the present. Now reality came flooding back — my hunger, Mom's injury, Cat.

Officer Hanston had never called me back.

"Come on in, Ross," Mom said.

The door opened fully and he stepped inside, clad in jeans and a black Rayne T-shirt, his scraggly hair in a ponytail. He carried two full McDonald's bags, which he handed to me. "Didn't know what breakfast stuff you'd want, so I got one of everything."

"Thanks." I took them from Ross's hand, my hunger doubling at the enticing scents wafting from the bags. Sinking down on my bed, I pulled out a breakfast burrito and unwrapped it.

Ross walked over to Mom. "How ya doing, Rayne?" He sat down in the chair I'd been using, half his profile to me.

I took a bite of the burrito and tasted the salty, velvet explosion of eggs and cheese.

Mom managed a smile. "I'm doing okay."

"Less pain?"

"Long as I don't move."

He patted her casted arm. "I sent Wendell down to bring up

your suitcases, Shaley's too. The car's at a delivery door. Reporters are still camped out at the main entrance."

"Thanks. What's happening with the band?"

"They're coming to see you soon." Ross turned to me. "Wendell told me you saw that photographer around here."

I swallowed a bite, reaching for my phone. "Yeah. I need to find out if they caught him."

Mom and Ross waited while I called Officer Hanston. They hadn't found Cat yet, he told me. Officers were still looking. I shot Ross a weary look and shook my head. "Okay, thanks. Please call me when you get him."

I ended the call and sighed. How could Cat hide so well? Everything within me still wanted to go out and find him myself. This was *stupid*, having to sit in this room and do nothing.

Ross gave me a look like he knew what I was thinking. "Sit tight, Shaley, they'll get him."

Yeah, yeah.

Breakfast didn't taste so good anymore. I finished the burrito and halfheartedly fished in the first McDonald's bag. I pulled out a blueberry muffin.

Ross cleared his throat. "When everybody gets here we need to have a meeting."

Mom's mouth twisted. "What's there to talk about? The tour's over."

Ross nudged his bottom lip upward, puckering his heavy chin. "Rayne, you can't blame yourself for what happened."

"If I'd just stayed in the limo ..."

"Oh, sure," I retorted. "How about if Cat had stayed away from us, like he was supposed to?"

Mom shook her head. "Shaley. Tell Ross what Jerry said."

"Jerry?" Ross raised his eyebrows.

"Later, Mom." I didn't want to have this conversation right now. Or ever. I picked up the blueberry muffin.

Ross looked from me to Mom. "What'd he say?"

"Just before he died, he whispered something in Shaley's ear. He said 'Your father sent me.'"

Oh, great.

"Your *father*? Who is the guy?"

Indignation banged around in my chest. All these years, Mom had kept that part of her life private, even from me. And now Ross expected an easy answer — just like that? No way, not before I'd heard the whole story myself.

"We don't know where he is now. Mom hasn't seen him since before I was born."

Ross's jaw hardened. I knew the look — protective manager. He smacked his palms against his legs. "What's his name?"

My fingers curled around the muffin. This wasn't fair.

"Gary Donovon," Mom said.

Ross mouthed the name to himself. "Why didn't you tell me what Jerry said, Shaley?"

"I didn't — "

"There was no time, Ross." Mom's voice sharpened. "We're telling you now."

"No time? This is important! We got a madman out there, wanting you hurt!" He looked from me to Mom like we were both crazy. "Have you heard from the police this morning? Did they find him yet?"

"I haven't told them yet, Ross. And it's not Mom's fault — she didn't even know till this morning. I was going to call them."

He gaped at me. "*How* could you not tell the police?"

"Leave her alone." Mom's face pinched. "She's going to tell them now, that's all that matters."

"All that — " Ross shoved to his feet, his cheeks reddening. He picked up the chair, strode to the far wall, and jammed it down. Then stomped back and glared at me, hands low on his hips. "All right, Shaley, tell me what's going on. Why did you keep this to yourself?"

"Ross — "

"Be quiet, Rayne!" He shot her a look, then his face softened. He shifted his weight. "Okay. You two have been through a lot. I'll chalk this up to your brains being on overload. But Shaley, *why* didn't you say anything?"

"Because I didn't believe Jerry." My voice sounded small. "I didn't *want* to believe him."

"That's it, you don't *want* to believe. Since I can be a little more objective, let me tell you what this means." Ross's voice rose. "I thought the danger to all of us was over once that killer was caught. Now I'm hearing Jerry didn't act alone. That there's a man out there somewhere who apparently has it in for you, Rayne, and at the very least wants to kidnap Shaley."

Mom's eyes slipped shut. Her expression mixed fear and exhaustion. "I know."

I threw the muffin into the McDonald's bag. Ross was right and I knew it, but I didn't want to face it. And I didn't like the accusations about my father coming from *him*. "Maybe Jerry wasn't even telling the truth. He lied about everything else."

Ross flung his hands up. "You want to take a gamble on that?"

No. But still ... The father I never knew was being taken away from me before I could hear his full story.

"Well, *I* sure don't." Ross jabbed a finger against his chest. "I'm in charge of this tour. Two people have already been murdered on my watch, Shaley. I don't care to see a third." He swiveled, paced two steps toward the wall, and pivoted back. "Now we're one bodyguard short, the tour's over, and I've got to get everyone home safely. We need two guards here, switching off for this room, and that leaves no one for everybody else. And *now* I hear there's still a killer out there!"

My body went hot. I dragged my fingers along the bed, scrunching up the covers. Why hadn't I thought about this? What if my silence had put other members of the band in danger?

A knock rapped against the door.

"Yes?" Ross snapped. I twisted around.

Wendell's head appeared. "I've got the first two suitcases —"

"Fine. Push 'em in and leave."

Surprise at the angry tone flicked across Wendell's face. He glanced at Mom, then opened the door wider and rolled in my two large bags. The door closed.

I glared at Ross. "You didn't have to be so mean to him. He saved my life, you know."

Ross flapped a hand in the air. "And *I'm* trying to save lives now." He yanked his cell phone from a front pocket and punched multiple buttons. "Detective Myner should have been looking for this Gary Donovon since last night. Now you can bet Donovon's seen the news and gone underground. We may have lost our chance —" His head jerked. "Yes, Detective, it's Ross Blanke. Shaley has something to talk to you about."

Ross marched over to me and held out the phone. "Tell him."

17

Perched stiffly on my hospital bed, I told Detective Myner everything. I wouldn't look at Ross, but I could feel his laser-like stare. When I apologized to the detective for lying, Ross sucked air through his teeth. He didn't know Detective Myner had asked me what Jerry whispered, and I'd replied it was nothing important.

My fingers cramped from gripping the cell phone so hard.

"All right." The detective didn't even sound mad. At least that was something. Ross was mad enough for two people. "Thanks for telling me, Shaley. We'll start running this down immediately. We'll find the guy."

Fear and wild hope shot through me. If they found my father, maybe I could see him.

But if he'd sent Jerry, why would I want to?

"Okay. Thanks." My voice dulled out. I just wanted to reverse the world three days — when I knew nothing about my father and could still dream he was a good, loving man.

"Can I talk to your mom for a minute?" the detective asked.

"Sure." I handed the phone to Mom.

The detective's voice filtered to my ears. He asked for the spelling of Donovon.

Mom told him, then listened. "I don't know. The last time I saw him was seventeen years ago."

All appetite for breakfast was gone. The smells coming from the McDonald's bag turned my stomach. No way was I going to hear the rest of the story about my father like this.

I thrust myself off the bed and made for the bathroom. Inside, I shut the door hard and locked it, closing out Mom's voice.

The bathroom looked cold and sterile. A shower with a seat. One sink. A floor of white tile. The toilet was handicapped-size. On the wall next to it ran a strong silver bar for support.

Eyes burning, I sat down on the closed toilet and put my head in my hands. Loneliness washed over me in waves. How had I gotten here, in this hospital room, so far from my home? Why had God let me lose three friends in the last few days, one of them turning out to be a traitor?

Now I was losing my dad — before I even knew him.

A tear plopped to the tile between my feet.

Remember, God is always watching. Carly's words from two days ago ran through my head. Yesterday I'd vowed to find the truth — all of it. The truth about my earthly father, and the heavenly Father whom Carly insisted loved me so much.

So much for the heavenly one. Today I sure didn't feel any closer to God.

Maybe if terrible things stopped happening, I'd have more time to think about him.

No, you wouldn't. You wouldn't think about him at all.

The thought echoed in my mind.

Three days ago I was waiting excitedly for Brittany to come. For two months we'd been on tour. And before that I'd been home, living the life of a famous rock star's daughter. All those times I'd never thought about God for a minute. Why?

Because things hadn't been hard enough to make me seek him.

I straightened, blinking away tears. Carly's story ran through my head. She lost her parents and had her heart broken by the man she loved. When she'd turned to God, her life hadn't gotten any better for a long time. But she'd had the strength to deal with it. Because *inside*, she'd changed.

A shiver ran down my back. I drew my arms across my chest. I needed to take a hot shower and wash my hair. Change clothes.

So much for the outside. *What about your inside, Shaley?*

My mouth twisted. This was kind of weird, thinking about God in a hospital bathroom.

But the thoughts wouldn't go away.

My hands slipped over my eyes. I felt pretty stupid. And small. But if God was "always watching," I suppose he knew that anyway.

"God," I whispered, "here I am. Could you help, please? I'm ... tired. And I need your strength — like Carly has. I'm ready to pay more attention to you, but I'm not even sure how to start. Could you show me, please?"

A hard knock sounded on the door. My head snapped up.

"Shaley." Ross's voice.

"Yeah?"

"You hiding in there?"

"Yeah, I'm hiding. And praying." *Take that, Ross.*

"Oh. Well, you can stop now. We're off the phone."

Stop what — hiding or praying? I almost laughed. "Okay."

"And the band's here."

Oh, great. Now I'd have to face everybody else. Ross would make me tell them too.

"Coming."

Leaning both hands on the sink, I stared at myself in the mirror. I looked like a half zombie, long faced, circles under my eyes. My hair a mess.

Voices and laughter filtered from the room.

All the years Mom refused to talk about my father — and now *everyone* would be hearing about him. I wanted him to myself. I wanted my dreams back.

Plastering a tight smile on my face, I opened the bathroom door.

ey, Shaley," Morrey called, echoed by Stan and Rich. Kim shot me a smile.

"Hi." I pushed a strand of hair off my face. "Be careful with my patient. I've been taking care of her all night."

"I'll bet." Kim shook her head at Mom. "Probably had to tie her to the bed to keep her down."

Mom managed a smile.

They milled around Mom, taking turns leaning down to give her a kiss, gently touching the bump on her head. Stan sat down in the chair by her bed and whipped out a Sharpie pen to sign her cast. "Rayne reigns!" he printed, and handed the pen to Kim. She tapped it against her chin, then wrote, "One broken wrist — for all the hearts you've broken."

Ross laughed.

I walked to my bed and sat down. Against the wall were the additional suitcases Mick had brought up. Made me tired just to look at them. I didn't have the energy to open mine and find clean clothes.

"How are you, Rayne?" Morrey crossed his tattooed arms. "In a lot of pain?"

"Only when I breathe."

Rich patted her shoulder.

Ross cleared his throat. "Okay, we've got to talk."

Everyone looked grim. They knew what was coming.

Morrey brought over the second wooden chair and placed it on

Mom's left. "Here, Kim." She sat down, leaving Morrey to stand by the window. I scooted toward the top of my bed as Rich and Stan joined me. My muscles felt like rocks. Was Ross going to tell them about Jerry?

Ross stood in front of the TV, weight on one leg and hands low on his hips. "Okay, first, as the five of us discussed last night at the hotel, we've got to end the tour. Rayne's got a long recovery, and Rayne" — he looked to Mom — "we all just want you to go home and rest."

"Yeah," Stan murmured. Morrey and Kim nodded their heads.

Ross glanced at the clock. "Soon as I leave here I'm getting on the horn to charter a plane back to LA. I'm hoping we can line one up by this evening. We'll pay the hotel rooms for another night so you'll all have a place to stay until the flight. I'll be staying here in Denver until Rayne's able to fly. Then Shaley and I will get her home."

Mom closed her eyes. "I can't believe this. I can't believe the tour's over."

"Neither can I." Kim ran a hand through her white-blonde hair. "But what's worse is you're in a hospital."

Ross rubbed his jaw. "We've got to figure out what to do about bodyguards. Mick and Wendell need to stay here with Rayne. But I don't like the idea of you all going home without a single guard. The media will be all over you."

"No they won't." Stan shrugged. "They're all camped out at the hospital's front door, waiting for Rayne." He threw her a teasing smile.

Ross sighed. "We've got another issue."

I flung a look at Mom. She glanced from Ross to me, sending me a silent signal — *It's okay.*

"It came up this morning with the detective." Ross shifted his weight. "They're running down a lead that came from Jerry himself, just before he died."

Ross repeated Jerry's words — keeping me out of it. My shoulders sagged with relief.

Kim gasped. " 'Your father sent me.' What does that *mean*?"

Everybody started talking at once. Ross threw his hands up. "Wait!"

I focused on the bottom of the pushed-back curtain hanging from the ceiling. Ross launched into his arguments: No way were we taking a gamble on this. As far as we were concerned, there was still a killer out there. And the whole group needed protection.

The discussion went on, but I closed my ears. Part of me wanted to leave the room. The other part worried what would be said in my absence. Once thing I did know — I'd had it with waiting. This was *my* father they were talking about. As soon as everyone left, Mom was going to tell me the rest of her story. I prayed I would hear something, *anything*, that would allow me to believe Gary Donovon was still a good man today.

Please, God, let Jerry be lying.

19

With two thousand dollars in cash bulging in his wallet, Franklin Borden caught a cab from the bank to the nearest Verizon outlet.

So many cell phones to choose from. He walked around the store, shaking his head at the new technology. The world sure had changed in eight years.

"Can I help you, sir?" A fresh-faced kid — couldn't be older than twenty-five — gave him a salesman's smile.

"Yeah. I need a phone. And a service plan."

The kid led Franklin around the walls of shiny phones in all colors. You no longer just spoke into the things. Now practically all of them took pictures and videos, and text-messaged. Some hooked to the Internet. Some had full keyboards like a computer.

"Don't need any of the fancy stuff." Franklin grabbed a model from its stand. "I'll take this one."

He waited impatiently as the salesman set up his service and phone number. "Your address?" the kid asked.

Franklin fished a piece of paper from his pocket. On it he'd written his new P.O. Box number and zip code. "Just got this." He read it off to the salesman. The kid wrote it down.

Cell phone in his pocket, Franklin walked out of the store. He'd have to charge the phone for a couple hours. That was a problem. He might need it today. Where to plug it in while he was on the move all afternoon?

Stifling hot sun beat down on him as he stood on the street, thinking. Memories of prison flashed in his head. Right now it would be about lunchtime. A guard would be opening his cell, letting him out. He'd be walking along with the other inmates, wishing for eyes in the back of his head, highly aware of what every man around him was doing. Nerves on fire, muscles twitching.

Franklin glanced to his left — and spotted a police car. He froze.

The car drew closer, then passed by. The cop inside never even looked at him. At the next corner the cop turned.

Franklin exhaled.

The cell phone weighted his pocket. He'd have to check in for his flight early. Find an outlet somewhere in the airport and plug the thing in.

Which left him little time for the rest of his business.

He would not get close to Shaley and Rayne looking like some jailbird. He needed new clothes and shoes, plus a haircut.

Two blocks up Franklin saw a cab. He stepped into the street and raised his hand.

"Take me to the nearest mall," he told the driver as he slid inside the car.

20

The meeting broke up. Morrey, Kim, Stan, and Rich milled around, kissing Mom and saying their good-byes. Each of them hugged me too.

A tour's end was supposed to be exciting. Mission accomplished, fans pleased — now for some much-needed rest. But cut off so suddenly, and under these circumstances, it just dragged everyone down.

It felt almost like someone had died.

I smelled a hint of Kim's spicy perfume as she drew me close. "'Bye, Shaley," she whispered. "See you back home."

Home. My throat tightened. In a few days I would actually be *home*.

"Yeah." I pulled back and gave her a wan smile. "See you there."

Morrey ran his hand through the top of his black hair. "Take good care of your mom, now."

"I will."

As the four band members slipped into the hall, Ross hung back. "Be there in a minute," he called. He motioned me toward a corner by the door.

Great. Now what?

Ross faced me, his back to Mom, and lowered his voice. "You can come back to the hotel with us if you want. The nurses are here to watch over her."

"I know. But — no. I need to stay."

"Okay." He poked his tongue against his cheek. Clearly, he had more to say. "You know the police are looking for your father."

I drew back. *Your father.* I didn't like the sound of those words, coming from Ross. As if the relationship-that-never-was linked me to the man responsible for three deaths.

My mouth firmed. "Detective Myner told me."

"He told me too. I talked to him after your mom did. I made sure it was top priority with him. It's not safe for any of us as long as that man's on the loose."

My gaze dropped to the floor. I knew it wasn't safe. I just didn't want to think about it.

"Shaley." Ross nudged up my chin. "Don't do anything stupid."

I screwed up my face. "Like what?"

"Like sneak out on your own. Like try to find answers the police should be finding."

So that was it. While I'd been hiding in the bathroom, he'd apparently heard it all from Mom. How I longed to know about my father. How I wouldn't let the subject drop. Violation and betrayal kicked around in my gut.

My arms folded. "And why would I do that?"

Ross's stare bored right into me. "You're a teenager. They're known to do stupid things."

"Yeah, well, in case you've forgotten, I don't have time for stupidity. I have to take care of Mom."

"I know." He held my gaze, silently hammering home his point. Then he backed up a step. "Okay, then."

Ross turned around. "Rayne, I'm outta here. I'll be at the hotel if you need me."

"Thanks, Ross. For everything."

With a tight smile aimed at me, he left.

I stood staring at the closed door, visualizing Ross and the band members walking down the hall, slipping out a back entrance into a limo. I'd wanted them gone. But now the room felt so empty and silent. And behind me in the bed lay a mother who'd talked about me.

"Shaley."

I faced her, my expression accusing.

"I had to tell him."

I shivered. Had it gotten colder in here? "Had to tell him what? That I just won't leave you alone about my own dad?"

Mom's eyebrows drew together. "I didn't say that. Ross came to his own conclusions. I just told him about what I know of your father."

"Hooray for Ross, hearing it all before me."

"He didn't hear everything. Just the basics. *You,* I want to hear it all."

I rubbed a hand across my forehead. "Well, now's as good a time as any." My voice edged, but I didn't care. I was so tired of this.

"Come on over and sit down."

As I crossed to the chair, Mom sighed. "I'm so sad about the tour."

"Me too."

I sat down, glancing at the clock. "Your lunch should be here soon."

"Oh, joy. More hospital food." She licked her lips. "What about yours?"

"I'll get something from the cafeteria."

"You can't go down there alone."

Air seeped up my throat. "Is this how it's going to be the rest of my life, Mom? Can't even go down an elevator in a *hospital* by myself?"

"No. Not forever. Just ... until we get this sorted out."

Great. And if the police didn't find Gary Donovon, then what?

I dropped into the chair. "So tell me — what made him go bad? What *happened* between you two?"

PART 6
Rayne 1992

21

What happened? I'll tell you. It started with one niggling question that grew and grew in my mind: why wouldn't Gary ever allow me to go to his house?

By mid-April we'd been dating for over four months and really loved each other. Every chance we had, we'd be together. In the halls between classes, before and after school. Gary worked a lot, but he'd drive me home before returning to his own house to change into work clothes. On weekends after he got off work, Gary would come to my house, either to hang out there or pick me up to go out with friends.

And at least twice a month, a white rose, wrapped in green cellophane and tied with a red ribbon, would be delivered to my door. In it would be a note, always the same.

"You are my white rose. I love you. Gary."

We talked about everything — except the one thing that ultimately would matter. Gary knew my deepest secrets. He knew about my longing to be a singer. The loneliness I felt over not having a father, or brothers and sisters. For all my popularity at school and my large group of friends, that loneliness could sometimes overwhelm me. When I had an argument with a girlfriend or my mom, Gary was there to listen. He'd let me talk it out, wait for me to calm down, then often say just the right thing I needed to hear. I learned to trust his insights.

For his part, Gary talked to me about his worries over his grandmother's health and his plans to study psychology in college.

He told me about his distrust of the popular crowd at school, which is why he'd held back from talking to me for so long. He tended to view such people as fake and shallow. I had to admit, with some people, he was right. But as he got to know me and my friends, he saw us more for what we really were — struggling, trying to make sense of the world, just like everyone else.

Still, there was a big piece of Gary I couldn't reach — his private life with his grandmother. No matter how I tried, how many questions I asked, he *would not* let me in.

At first I pouted that he was ashamed of me. "Don't want your grandma Donovon to see me, huh? What am I, too ugly? Too fat?"

"You know you're the most beautiful thing on earth," he'd reply, and kiss my questions away.

By February I'd decided his grandmother didn't exist. He lived alone, and he'd made her up so I wouldn't feel sorry for him. The pictures he'd shown me of a sweet-faced, gray-haired woman were of some lady who lived down the street.

The first time I told Gary my theory, he laughed. "Rayne, you sure can be crazy sometimes."

But he still wouldn't take me to his house.

I would be turning sixteen in early May, which meant I'd *finally* get my driver's license. My mom had promised me her old Nissan. She was going to buy a new car. Well, used, but new to her. "Wait till I get my own car," I teased Gary one Saturday night as we drove away from my house. "I just might go see your grandmother on my own while you're at work."

Gary tensed. "Why do you keep coming back to my grandmother?"

"Maybe because I've never *met* her? I've never once seen your house?"

His lips firmed into a tight line. Suddenly, driving down a familiar street required his most rapt attention.

I folded my arms. "So what do you think? Will she like me?"

"Rayne." His voice hardened. "*Don't* go by my house. *Ever.*"

I stared at him. He had never spoken to me in such a harsh tone. "Why? You know everything about me, Gary Donovon. You've seen my house and my mother a million times, and she loves you to death. You say you love me. But you won't even let me meet the one other important person in your life. Just what are you hiding? For all I know, you've got a wife at home."

"Don't be stupid."

"Well, what am I *supposed* to think?"

"You're supposed to trust me."

"Trust you with what, Gary? To not give me answers? Not tell me the truth?"

He gripped the steering wheel. "Trust me when I say there's good reason to keep you away."

Maybe I should have been more understanding. But after four months of this, I was just plain frustrated. "Fine. I will trust you. Just tell me the reason."

"Rayne, I don't — "

"Tell me, Gary!"

He smacked his palm against the wheel. "*Why* do we have to go into this now? We're headed to a party, I've worked all day. Why can't we just have a good time?"

"Because this isn't just 'now,' that's why. You've been hiding something from me ever since we started dating. And no matter how much I pour my heart out to you, you still hold back. You want to know how that makes me feel? Like you don't *care* about me enough to think I'll understand."

A light in front of us turned red. Gary braked hard. He wouldn't look at me.

Okay. I'd had it. "Gary, if you don't tell me right now, you can just take me home."

His eyes narrowed. The line of his jaw turned to granite. "Fine, Rayne." His shoulders dropped. When he spoke again, his voice was thick with resignation. "Maybe I just should then."

Fear for him stabbed through my anger. I'd never heard him

sound so depressed. I touched his shoulder. "Please tell me. What is it?"

He focused on the light. It turned green. He hit the accelerator.

I sat twisted in his direction, not taking my eyes off him. And I *wouldn't* stop staring until he answered my question.

Gary sighed. "My neighborhood's . . . not safe."

"What do you mean?"

He shook his head. "There are some nasty people living around me."

I processed this. "Then why do you live there?"

"It's my grandmother's home. There's no place else to go."

"Why don't you sell it and move somewhere else?"

His face darkened. "Rayne, drop it, okay? You *don't* know what you're talking about."

"I was just—"

"I said drop it!"

I turned away and slammed back against my seat. Anger wafted from me in waves. We simmered all the way to the party, not saying a word to each other. All evening we stayed on opposite ends of the room, talking to other people.

The ride back to my house was quiet.

We didn't make up for four days.

After that, for the next three weeks until I got my license and car, we talked and hung out, trying to be with each other like before. But things weren't the same. You've heard the saying about the elephant in the room no one will talk about? That's what it felt like. This giant *thing* sat between us—and neither of us wanted to face it. But I knew we couldn't last this way. I felt cut to the core that he wouldn't tell me what was wrong.

As the days wore on, that hurt turned to doubt. If Gary couldn't trust me with this, why should I trust him? Maybe he was involved in something he didn't want me to know about.

Sometimes even now I wonder what would have happened if I hadn't taken matters into my own hands. If only I could have seen the future then. Maybe everything would have turned out differently.

But of course, I had no crystal ball. And so, burning with the need to know, after my sixteenth birthday I did exactly what Gary warned me never to do. Armed with my new license, behind the wheel of my Nissan, I drove to his house one Saturday while he was at work.

22

I only meant to drive *by* Gary's house. Just to get a feel for things.

He'd said the neighborhood wasn't "safe." At first it didn't seem that way to me as I cruised the nearby streets. The houses were small and wooden, probably with two to three bedrooms. Older. Lawns weren't full of weeds, but neither were they perfectly groomed. I saw plenty of trees and bushes. Lots of cars parked in driveways and at the curb.

It didn't hit me until I was on Gary's street: this should be an area full of children. But I didn't see one toy in a front yard, or bikes lying on the sidewalks.

Gary's address was number 423. On my right the houses at 413, 415, 417 drifted by. Three doors up I spotted his house, painted off-white with teal trim. A compact front porch with three steps. It looked well-kept and was the only house around with flowers in the yard.

On her knees, weeding in those flower beds, was Gary's grandmother.

I recognized her immediately — the curly gray hair and round, pleasant face. She worked slowly but with deliberate movements, as if the task was a challenge she enjoyed. I knew she'd been weak a lot lately from her heart. It was surprising she was outside at all.

Automatically I slowed, drinking in the sight of her through my open passenger window. In person she looked even more friendly and kind than in her pictures. I wanted to know her. I wanted her to know me.

She looked up as I rolled by—and our eyes met.

Surprise flicked across her brow. One hand, holding a trowel, rose. "Rayne?"

My foot poised above the brake.

For a split second I stared at her, heart pounding. She must have seen pictures of me. Now what? I couldn't just drive on and ignore her. But if she told Gary I'd been here ...

I pulled over to the curb and put the car in park. The next thing I knew I was on the pavement, walking toward her with a smile plastered on my face. Did *she* know I wasn't supposed to be here?

"My goodness, Rayne." Grandma Donovon dropped her gardening tool and struggled to her feet. "What a nice surprise." She started toward me on gimpy legs. "Oh, my." She shook her head. "I've been kneeling too long."

"Hi." I reached a hand out to her, my smile stretching to genuine. "It's so good to finally meet you." She couldn't have been over five feet tall. I could feel the warmth emanating from her tiny frame.

Grandma Donovon batted away my hand and reached for a hug instead. "And it's wonderful to meet *you*." She gripped me hard, then stepped back, looking me over with her chocolate-brown eyes. "You're even prettier in person. Didn't think that could be possible. Although Gary's told me it's true."

I laughed, feeling self-conscious. And guilty. Gary had been bragging about me—and here I was, showing up on his doorstep behind his back.

For an awkward moment Grandma Donovon and I stared at each other, as if she read my mind.

Her gaze flicked next door, then across the street. I followed her glances but saw no one. She smiled again and wiped her brow. "What brings you here? Gary's at work, you know."

I pulled my bottom lip between my teeth. "Oh. Yeah. I thought so, but ... I drove by just in case I'd see his truck ..."

My words ran out. Grandma Donovon nodded, but her eyes clouded. She knew I was lying. Unspoken emotions vibrated between us. From me, curiosity — what had Gary been hiding? From her — fear.

Why would she be afraid?

At the next house over a screen door squeaked. Grandma Donovon's eyes snapped toward it. A guy maybe twenty-five years old slouched through the door and down two steps to the scruffy yard. His cold stare fixed on Grandma Donovon. He wore baggy jeans with holes in the knees and a faded blue T-shirt. His blond hair scraggled to his shoulders in wild dreadlocks. Behind him trailed two more guys about the same age, one with short dark hair and another with a totally shaved head. Everything about the three of them, from their hard faces to the cocky way they moved, reeked of hate and evil.

They lined up on their sidewalk, legs apart, arms folded — and stared at us.

I gawked back at them, feeling hairs rise on the back of my neck. I wanted to run to the car but couldn't begin to move.

"Rayne." Grandma Donovon's voice dropped to a forced calm. "I think you'd better — "

"Well, now." Dreadlocks let out a low whistle aimed at me. "Who do we have here?"

My breath shallowed. I glanced nervously at Grandma Donovon, seeking a cue. I couldn't just walk away from this. Somehow I sensed she'd pay.

"Just a friend, Bart." Grandma Donovon tried to sound nonchalant but failed. "She was just leaving." Her eyes cut to me, two high spots of color on her cheeks. *Go*, her expression warned.

"No she ain't." Bart started a slow saunter toward us, hands sliding into his pockets. As if he had all the time in the world to get to us, knowing we wouldn't dare move. "I got to see this *vision* of *beauty* up close." The two other guys trailed behind him.

My veins chilled. I pulled both arms across my chest, watching them draw near me like I was some trapped animal. By the time

Bart stood on Grandma Donovon's sidewalk, mere feet away, my insides shook.

Bart's mouth twisted into a smile. "I like this." His eyes dropped down the length of me, then slowly rose back to my face. He nodded. "Yeah. I like this very much."

His friends grunted and grinned, enjoying my fear.

Bart rocked back on his heels. "You a friend of Gary's?"

My tongue stuck to the roof of my mouth. Grandma Donovon stepped in front of me. "Leave her alone, Bart."

He snorted. "Oh, what, Granny, you gonna make me stop?"

Her mouth pressed tight. "You've got no business with her, she was just driving by." She turned to me firmly. "Good-*bye*."

"No, no." Bart swiped out his hand and caught my arm. His palm felt hot.

I yanked away. Who did these guys think they were? "Let go of me!"

Bart's expression blackened. One side of his mouth curled up, his eyes slitting. "Don't you know I own this neighborhood?" He jerked his head toward Baldy. "Go get her license plate."

Air hissed between Grandma Donovon's teeth. Baldy strode toward my car, pulled a small notebook and pen from his deep front pocket, and jotted down the plate. He sauntered back and handed the paper to Bart.

"There ya go." Bart read it over then stuck it in his pocket. He aimed a slow smile at Grandma Donovon and me. "You can go now, Blondie. We got your plate. Soon we'll know — "

An engine gunned on the street. We all turned toward it to see Gary in his truck, hunched over the wheel and teeth clenched. My heart sank to my toes. What was he doing home so early?

Gary surged into the driveway and screeched to a stop. He got out of his truck and slammed the door. He walked toward us stiffly, fear and determination and protectiveness tightening his face.

Bart sniggered. He no longer had to question how I knew Gary.

"What's going on?" Gary drew up, lasering me with an accusing look — *now you've done it*. He turned suspicious eyes on Bart.

"Nothin', man." Bart shrugged. "Just getting to know your girl-friend. Oh." He pulled the piece of paper from his pocket. "And writing this down." He flashed the license plate number at Gary. "In case you give us any trouble."

Gary's jaw worked back and forth. His fingers curled toward his palms. For a minute nobody moved.

Across the street a door banged. Four guys, a little older than the three around us, filed out, brewing with menace. "You got trouble over there?" one of them called.

"Nah." Bart gave me a smile that turned my stomach. "We're just gettin' acquainted with Gary's girlfriend."

"Oh. Didn't know he had one." The guy laughed, and Bart chuckled with him.

Goosebumps skittered down my arms. What had I done by coming here?

The four across the street milled in their yard, watching us. Lewd comments drifted across the pavement.

Gary glared at me. "Go home." His voice could have cut steel.

My lips parted, but no words came. If I left — then what? The guys all looked like they were aching to jump Gary and beat him up. Seven to one. Strong as he was, he couldn't possibly stand up to that.

Gary ground his teeth. "*Go.*" He dug fingers into my elbow and pushed me toward my car.

Heart in my throat, I swiveled and scurried down the sidewalk. The guys across from us whistled and catcalled. For a terrifying minute I thought they would come over and surround me. I yanked open my car door, slipped inside, and slammed down the locks.

My hands shook as I turned the key in the ignition.

As I drove away I peered into the rearview mirror and saw Bart all up in Gary's face, shaking a finger at him and ranting. The two guys near him — and the four across the street — watched, sneering. Gary just stood there, taking it, one hand clutching his grand-mother's shoulder.

Panic washed over me. How could I leave him? What if they did beat him up?

My foot lifted from the accelerator, reaching for the brake.

Gary's head turned toward my car. The sheer pleading in his expression shocked me. *Leave, Rayne*, it cried. *Please leave!*

I knew then that if I went back, it would only get worse. Whoever these people were, whatever evil power they had over Gary—I'd just given them more fuel for their fire.

Worst of all was the shame I saw on Gary's face. I'd seen him in his weakest moment, unable to stand up to these bullies. To him, that was more punishment than a physical beating.

As I turned the corner and he faded from sight, I wondered if he would ever forgive me.

PART 7
Monday 2009

23

A nurse appeared in the hospital room doorway, carrying a lunch tray. Mom's story abruptly stopped.

Through sheer willpower I pulled myself back to the present, Mom's last words swirling in my head. What had *happened* to my father after she drove away?

Biting back impatience, I took the tray and set it on the rolling table by Mom's bed. I uncovered the food and unwrapped the silverware. She had baked chicken and vegetables. A salad. Didn't look a bit appetizing to me, but my stomach growled anyway.

What I wanted was pizza.

Mom stared at her food dully.

"You want to sit up more?" I reached for the button on the bed.

"Yeah. Thanks."

She winced as we got her sitting up straighter. Lines zigzagged across her forehead. She needed sleep. Remorse panged through me. All that pain — and here I was, pushing her to tell me about my father.

I filled her water glass. Mom ate in silence.

"Is it any good?" I made a face at the food.

"It's all right."

I focused on my cell phone, lying on my bed. "Wanna order out? We can get pizza delivered."

Mom set down her fork. "Yeah. That sounds great." She pushed the rolling table back. "Get this thing away from me."

"You bet."

I set the tray out in the hall. Wendell just shook his head at me.

Back in the room I dialed information and found a nearby take-out for pizza. We ordered an extra large pepperoni and mushroom, with Coke and paper plates. I put the cost and a tip on my credit card, then told Wendell a delivery would be coming.

I tossed my cell phone back on my bed. Ran both hands through my hair. "You want to take a nap before it comes, Mom?"

"No. Afterward. Then I won't have anything to wake me up."

I snorted. "Except doctors and nurses and who knows what."

She smiled weakly.

My arms folded as I gazed at her, unwilling to push for more of the story.

She flicked a look at the ceiling. "Okay, Shaley. Come on back and sit down. I know what you're thinking."

"You sure it's okay?"

"What else am I going to do, turn somersaults?"

My cell phone rang. I picked it off my bed and checked the ID. The number and name had been blocked. I stared at the cell, deciding whether to answer. Something made me push the *talk* button.

"Hello?"

"Shaley." A man's voice. Hard.

"Yeah?"

"This is Len Torret."

Cat!

"Got news for you," he said. "I got a picture of you and your bodyguard lover outside your mom's hospital room door. You two were looking pretty cozy."

What? It took a minute to realize what he was talking about. My jaw sagged open, but no words came. I sank down on my bed.

"*Cashing In*'s gonna pay me fifty thousand for it. I'm offering it to you first for seventy-five."

My back stiffened. "How *dare* you try to blackmail me! You don't have any picture of me anyway."

"Who is it?" Mom demanded.

"Oh yeah?" Cat sneered. "Then how do I know you and that bodyguard were hugging? I looked around a corner on your floor — and there you were."

"If you looked around the corner, you saw me fighting him first. I was trying to come after *you* and he wouldn't let me."

"Nice story. Tell it to the public when the photo's published."

Rage catapulted up my spine. I shoved to my feet. Cat would've had to zoom in for a close-up from that far away. And he'd obviously waited for the perfect shot to spread his lies.

"You want the photo or not, Shaley? You pay for it, it doesn't get published."

"I'm not paying you a dime!"

"Last chance."

"Forget it! And I can't wait to see you in jail. Just wait till everybody sees a picture of *that*." I punched off the call and threw the phone on my bed.

"Shaley, who was that?" Mom's voice was sharp.

I bent over and put my face in my hands. My cheeks flamed at the thought of that picture printed for everybody to see. And it wouldn't be by itself. Oh, no. *Cashing In* would make up a whole embarrassing story about Wendell and me. Wouldn't matter that none of it was true.

How could I ever face Wendell again?

"Shaley!"

I lifted my head, my eyes burning. "It was Cat." My voice cracked. I told Mom what he'd said.

Her face turned crimson. I knew only the pain kept her from jumping out of bed. "Where's my cell phone?"

"In your purse."

"Give it to me; I'm calling that policeman you talked to."

I pulled it from her purse and handed it to her. It was still on, half charged. Mom pressed the number for Officer Hanston as I read it off my own phone. Pacing the room, I listened to her berate him for not finding Cat when he'd been so close to us. "Now he's trying to blackmail my daughter. This is just ridiculous!"

She listened for a minute, steaming, then thrust the phone toward me. "Here. He wants to talk to you."

"I don't *want* to talk to him."

"You want Cat caught or not? *Take* it."

Sick to my stomach, I took the cell. I wanted to throw it out the window. I wanted to be anything but the daughter of somebody famous at that moment. How tiring it was living in a fishbowl! Now I'd have to explain that whole scene between Wendell and me to this policeman, to Ross and the other band members, and all my friends. If only I could crawl into a cave and hide.

My tone flat, I told Officer Hanston what had happened with Wendell, and about the picture Cat claimed to have. And how he wanted me to pay him not to print it.

"I'm sorry this happened," Officer Hanston said. "We'll keep looking for him. He's probably left the hospital now, but at least we know he's in the area."

Yeah, he'd left all right — to print off the picture he'd taken. I tried to tell myself maybe it would come out too dark without a flash. But he'd have all kinds of ways to lighten a dark photo.

When the call ended I tossed down my phone and exchanged a searing look with Mom.

"I'm sorry, Shaley." She sounded so tired.

"It's not your fault."

She tried to smile. "The price you pay for being my daughter."

I shrugged.

Mom shifted her head, pain flicking across her face. "Let me tell you some more of my story before the pizza gets here."

She was trying to get my mind off things. I ran a hand across my forehead. Could I even concentrate enough to listen?

"Come on, Shaley. Don't you want to know what happened?"

Of course I did. But my head was in such a whirlwind, blown

between the present and the past. What was I going to do when that picture was released?

I took a deep breath and blew it out. Tiredly, I walked to the chair beside Mom's bed and sat down. "Yes. I want to know."

PART 8
Rayne 1992

24

That Saturday night, Gary and I were supposed to go out to a movie. I called his house three times to check on him, scared to death he was lying in some hospital, beat to a pulp.

No one answered.

Limbs shaking, I dressed for our date. I told myself he was all right. He was just too ashamed and mad to talk to me. Tears burned my eyes, and my breath came in little puffs. My mom was out with friends, and the house felt as silent and cold as a tomb.

As the eternal minutes ticked by, the fear inside me grew claws. Maybe Gary wouldn't show up at all. How could I make it through the whole night, not knowing what had happened to him?

By 7:00, when he was supposed to arrive, I paced my room, hands clutched to my chest. Every sound in the street made me jump.

If he did show, no way could we go to a movie tonight. I wouldn't hear a word of it. We needed to talk.

If he'd ever talk to me again.

Gary pulled up to our curb at 7:10. Cold relief nearly sank me to the floor.

I grabbed my purse and ran out the door. Gary was just reaching the sidewalk when I flew down the porch steps. I ran to meet him and threw myself against his chest.

"I'm sorry." I clutched the front of his shirt, crying into his neck. "I'm so sor-ry."

He held me for a minute, his muscles stiff. I could hear the anger in each of his breaths.

"Come on." He nudged me away, glancing around for the curious eyes of neighbors. "Let's get off the yard."

"Mom's not home." I wiped my face. "Come inside."

In the house, he made sure the front door locked behind us. We sank down on the couch. Gary hunched over, forearms on his legs and hands clasped. He stared at the blue carpet, his face dark and brooding. I was afraid to speak. Afraid he'd just snap and walk out the door.

Huddled against the arm of the couch, I waited him out.

He rocked his hands up and down. "I told you not to come, Rayne." He spoke to his feet.

"I know. I'm *so sorry.*"

He closed his eyes and shook his head.

I waited for a long minute for him to say more.

"Gary, what —"

"Do you know what you've done?" The words burst from him. His head swiveled toward me. "Now they've got me worse than ever. They already threaten my grandmother. I already have to do whatever they say so they won't hurt her or the house. Now they've got *you.*" His face twisted until I couldn't bear it.

I sank my fingers into his arm. "Who *are* they?"

He turned back toward the floor. His brows knit. "Ever hear of the Westrock Gang?" His voice sounded dull, defeated. He knew my answer.

Air pooled in my throat. No. This couldn't be *them.* Westrock was the toughest Caucasian gang in Southern California. Its tentacles reached through the state and up the West Coast. These criminals, these *animals,* were in the news all the time for running drugs and killing innocent people. Anyone who got in their way could be killed.

"Who hasn't?" I whispered.

"Well, you just met three of its members."

I didn't know what to say. For a minute I just stared at him. "And the four guys across the street?"

"Oh yeah. You've met seven."

Thoughts whirled in my brain until I could barely think. "How did they ... why are they on your street?"

Gary pushed out a strained laugh. "They have to live somewhere. And wherever that is, they take over the neighborhood. It's the only reason they can get away with all they do. Neighbors might get nosy with all the people coming to the house day and night for drugs. They might call the cops to turn down the noise at late-night parties. But if you've got every neighbor under your thumb, if you threaten to trash their house, take their kids, *kill their grandmother* — they're likely to leave you alone."

Kill their grandmother? Fear uncoiled in the pit of my stomach. "You mean they've threatened to hurt Grandma Donovon?"

Gary nodded. He still wouldn't look at me.

I turned away from him, stared across the living room. The mere imagining of Gary's fear broke me out in sweat. How did he sleep at night? How did he leave his house for a *minute*?

"Why don't you sell the house and move away?"

Gary raised his head and pressed back against the couch. "We've tried, Rayne. Don't you think we'd do anything to get out from under this?"

"What happened when you tried?"

Gary's chin jutted out. "The 'for sale' sign on our yard lasted one day. When I got home from school, it was torn to pieces and scattered on the street. Bart, the leader from next door, was *in my house*. Sitting on the couch with my grandmother, having a 'friendly chat' about how we were such good neighbors, they didn't want to lose us. How, if we tried to sell our house again, they'd pay us a visit in the middle of the night."

My mouth creaked open. "They'd ... kill you?"

"Oh, probably not *me*," he said bitterly. "That would be too easy, wouldn't it. They'd beat me till I never walked again. After making me watch what they did to my grandmother — *before* they stuck a knife in her heart."

My throat closed up. Gary's face blurred. I thought of all the times he'd sat staring into space in French class before we started dating. The way he'd walk down the hall, hardly noticing anyone around him. No wonder he'd kept to himself. The *weight* that must be on his shoulders.

This couldn't be real.

"Gary, I'm so … I just can't …"

He swallowed hard.

"I've done it now, haven't I." Guilt burned in my chest. I reached out to him, closing my hands around his wrist. "You didn't want them to see me."

His jaw moved back and forth. "They took your license plate number. They've got dirty cops on their payroll. All they have to do is ask one to run your plate and give them your address. Now they know where you live. It's just one more thing they can threaten me with."

My veins turned to ice. I wasn't even sure who I was more scared for — me and Mom, or Gary. "Would they come here?"

"If they have to." Gary pulled away from me and stood. "Now it's *my* job to make sure they don't."

I slumped against the couch, staring up at him, my fingers digging into my jeans. There was more, I knew it.

"What do you mean?" The words barely squeezed out of my mouth.

He swung away from me, a sick look on his face.

"Gary?" I bounced to my feet and caught his arm. Slowly, he rotated to face me.

"They've got jobs they want me to do, Rayne, okay?"

"What kind of jobs?"

"Delivering drugs. Collecting money."

My jaw dropped. "You can't do that! You could go to *jail*."

"Yeah, and my grandmother and you can get killed if I don't."

"But this — No. No way. You have to go to the police."

"Really?" He glared at me. "And how do I know which cop won't run right to the gang and tell them? And even if I do get an honest one, then what? I'd have to tell the police everything I've seen, testify against gang members. You think I'd live through that?"

My fingers slipped from his skin. I stepped back, weak-kneed. This was a nightmare. "There has to be *something* you can do."

"Oh, good. Tell me what."

"I don't know. *Something.*"

"There *isn't*, Rayne. I was trapped before, but things were going okay as long as I kept my mouth shut like the rest of the neighborhood. But they've been harder on me from the beginning, because I'm just the right age to recruit. They need fresh blood to do their dirty work. Now *you've* shown up. The minute you left, Bart announced he had a 'favor' for me to do. Since he was 'kind enough' to let you leave."

I dropped my face into my hands. I just wanted to fall to the floor. What had I done to Gary? I'd give anything to turn back time and change that drive to his house.

But it was too late. Gary couldn't tell Bart no. He couldn't go to the police. He and his grandmother couldn't leave the neighborhood. As I stood there, trembling, crying into my palms, I looked down the future and saw nothing but terror for Gary. And I couldn't stand it. Couldn't bear to think what I had done.

At that moment I knew somehow, some way, I had to reverse the damage I'd caused. I had to find Gary a way out of this.

PART 9
Monday 2009

25

M ale voices rose from the hospital hallway. Wendell, talking to someone.

The pizza had arrived.

I pushed from the chair and headed for the door to take the box from Wendell. Just seeing his face brought back all my rage against Cat. At least Wendell didn't know about the picture yet. He brought in the soft drinks and plates. The pizza smelled great, but I barely noticed. My thoughts bounced all over the place.

I'd never dreamed Mom had lived through such a nightmare. Had my father done some 'favor' for that gang — and ended up running from the cops?

What if it wasn't his fault at all? Maybe he really was a good man. And Jerry had lied. I so wanted to believe that.

"We got extra for you, Wendell." I set the box on my bed. "And here's a Coke."

"Great. Thanks."

I took out two pieces each for me and Mom, and left the rest for Wendell, which was a lot. With all those muscles burning fuel, he'd have no problem eating it. He returned to the hallway, carrying the pizza box and his Coke. I took Mom her plate.

The first bite of pizza burst in my mouth with flavor. Hot, salty, spicy.

Mom and I ate in silence.

As I finished my second piece my cell phone rang. I tensed.

Leaning over my bed, I focused on the ID. *Detective Myner.* My breath hitched. Had he found my father?

I wiped off my greasy hand and picked up the phone. "Hello."

"Hi, Shaley, Detective Myner here." Muted voices rumbled in the background. Sounded like he was in a noisy office. "Hope you don't mind me using your cell number. The hospital's not letting any calls through to your Mom's room." He chuckled. "Probably half the callers are claiming to be police officers."

"Yeah. That's okay."

"I promised to call as soon as I learned anything about your father."

I sat down on my bed, stiff-backed. To Mom I whispered, "They've found something."

Please, God, let me hear Jerry lied!

"Okay." My voice sounded small.

"We don't know everything yet," the detective said. "But we have traced where he went when he left California. And, more important, we know who he became."

26

In a whirlwind hour of activity Franklin Borden had bought new pants, a shirt, belt, wallet, new watch, and shoes. He put them on in a store bathroom and stuffed his old clothes in the trash, followed by the paper bag of possessions he'd been carrying around all day.

There. Now he looked like anybody else.

He slipped his cell phone and charger into his pocket.

Next on his list — a haircut at the mall's drop-in salon.

A half hour later, Franklin emerged looking and feeling like a new man. He checked his watch. He needed to hurry to the airport and plug in his cell phone.

In the cab he couldn't sit still. His fingers drummed both knees, his head swiveling from one window to the other. Plans bounced around his head like pinballs.

He *would* get to Rayne and Shaley — today. Didn't matter if they had a lot of security around them. He'd find a way.

Franklin's cab pulled up at the airport. He paid the driver and strode for the United counter. There he paid for his ticket. He made it through security and headed for his gate. In a corner he found an outlet, where he plugged in his phone.

Franklin settled into a chair to wait. That's one thing prison taught a man — how to wait. His watch read 1:45. The flight would leave in two hours.

27

What do you mean, who he became?" I asked Detective Myner. Mom watched me intently, her pizza forgotten. It occurred to me I should hand her the phone and let her hear the news first. I'd been longing to know about my father for years. *She'd* been wondering about where he'd gone even before I was even born.

But the phone glued to my fingers.

Detective Myner cleared his throat. "Our tracing began with the man you knew as Jerry Brand. As I told your mom yesterday, while running his fingerprints through our system we discovered he was living under an alias. His real name was Jerry Rostand. Rostand was in an Arizona prison until his release earlier this year. His cellmate was a man named Franklin Borden."

"Franklin Borden." I raised my eyebrows at Mom — *ever hear of him?*

She shook her head.

"Borden is a legal name," the detective said. "It was granted through the courts some seventeen years ago. This man's birth name was Gary Donovon."

Heat rolled through my limbs. I couldn't move. My father was in *prison* with Jerry?

All my hopes and prayers that Jerry had lied melted away. My father was in prison. And if he'd been in a cell with Jerry, he'd have known exactly what kind of man Jerry was.

"Shaley, you there?"

"Y-yeah. That's him. Gary Donovon."

"What happened to him?" Mom demanded. "Where is he?"

I moved the phone away from my mouth. "In prison."

Her eyes slipped shut.

I swallowed hard and spoke into the cell again. "What did he do?"

"Armed robbery. He went in eight years ago."

Armed robbery. I curled my fingers into my palm. At least it wasn't murder. "What ... I mean, how did he ... do it?"

"He held up a night clerk at a convenience store."

"*Why?*"

Detective Myner hesitated. "Shaley, I don't know why criminals do what they do."

Criminals. The pizza turned sour in my stomach. I shouldn't have answered this call. I didn't want truth now. I just wanted to hear the rest of Mom's story — when Gary Donovon was the victim, not the bad guy.

A new thought blew through my head. "Have you called him in prison? Asked him why he sent Jerry?"

The detective sighed. "Turns out we just missed him. Franklin Borden was released yesterday."

Tingles pranced around the back of my neck. "Yesterday? Then where is he?"

"We don't know." Detective Myner tried to sound factual, but I could hear the concern beneath his words. "He served all his time and got out with no parole, so he was free to go where he wanted. We've got officers working on tracking him down. He didn't seem to have any relatives in the area, so it's like looking for a needle in a haystack. But we'll keep on it. Soon as I hear anything further, I'll let you know."

We missed him by one day? Now what if he couldn't be found at all? "You mean you have no idea where he is?"

"Afraid not. But we're working on it."

Working on it. Great. Just like the Denver police were "working" on finding Cat.

"Yeah, okay. Thanks." In a daze I hit the *end* button and laid my phone on the bed.

"What'd he say?" Mom gripped the top of her covers.

I told her.

Mom stared at the wall, trying to process it all. A silent minute ticked by. Slowly, a revelation dawned on her face. "Eight years, you said? He went to prison eight years ago?"

I nodded.

Mom's eyes closed. She turned her head away, chin lowering. Her right hand drifted up to a fist at the base of her neck.

"Mom, what is it?"

Some time passed before she spoke. "Eight years ago, the white roses stopped coming."

PART 10
Rayne 1992

28

That summer before my junior year of high school was the best and worst of my life. The best, because when I was with Gary, nothing else mattered. I believed we could conquer the world. And I knew we would always stay together. But even as our love grew and white roses continued to arrive at my door, a part of Gary drew away from me. He refused to talk about the "favors" he had to do for Bart and his friends so the Westrock gang would leave Gary's grandmother and me alone.

"Don't worry about it," he'd say whenever I asked. "I have it worked out."

On the surface, apparently he did. No one bothered me. No one bothered his house. Life went on.

I tried to tell myself nothing was happening. Idle threats from Bart, that's all Gary had heard. But Gary's moodiness, the occasional faraway look in his eyes, and mostly his tense muscles whenever a cop passed us on the street screamed the truth.

Still, what I couldn't see was easy to deny.

Then on August twenty-ninth, a little over one week before school started, the world came crashing down.

It was a Saturday night. Gary had worked all day and was picking me up for an end-of-summer party at Christy's house at eight o'clock.

The night was hot. I was dressed in jeans, a red sleeveless top, and red heels. Gary kissed me when I answered the door and gave me his wonderful crooked smile. "You look terrific."

"So do you."

Gary looked happy, ready to have a good time. For the past few weeks he'd been like that. I figured the troubles with his neighbors really had come to an end.

He grabbed my hand as we walked down the porch steps and sidewalk. The sun had gone down, night settling around us and lights snapping on in my neighbors' windows. We slipped inside his truck, laughing about some silly thing that had happened at his job.

Two miles from my house, I noticed his eyes flitting nervously to the rearview mirror.

"What's wrong?" I started to glance over my shoulder.

"Don't look back. I think somebody's following us."

I stiffened. "Who?"

He wouldn't answer.

We turned a corner. It took all my willpower not to look behind me. "Are they still there?"

"Yeah." His fingers curled around the steering wheel.

The next ten minutes seemed to take forever. Every turn we made, the car stuck with us.

"What do they *want*?" I gripped the edge of the seat.

Gary just shook his head.

We turned off the busy main street into Christy's residential neighborhood. One block later an engine gunned, and a black car swerved up alongside us. A bald guy in the passenger seat motioned Gary to pull over. I recognized him. One of Bart's friends.

Gary's whole body stiffened. I could feel the indecision oozing from him. Refusing to obey would be dangerous. But he didn't want me anywhere near these guys.

All my weeks of convenient denial melted. Westrock hadn't been leaving Gary alone at all. He'd just managed to keep it from me.

His jaw set. "Rayne, don't say a word. Don't even look at them. Hear me?"

He pulled to the curb. I heard the car park behind us, its engine still running. Footsteps approached — more than one person. My heart rammed against my ribs. I focused on my feet.

Gary got out of his truck and shut the door.

"You were supposed to come over before you left." The voice filtered through Gary's closed window. It was mean and hard — one I hadn't forgotten.

Bart.

"Nobody told me that," Gary said.

"You got a short memory, Donovon. My boy here told you. Right, Andy?"

"Yeah."

Silence. I could hear the lie in Andy's voice. Or was this some set-up of Bart's?

Barely moving my head, I slid a look toward the window. Gary stood with his back to it, as if shielding me from them. Over his shoulder I could see Bart.

Gary made a sound in his throat. "What do you want?"

Bart spat on the street. "A delivery."

"When?"

"Now."

"I'm busy right now. Can we do this later?"

"Since when do you put me off?" Bart shoved his face in Gary's.

Gary didn't flinch. "Since I'm not alone. I thought you wanted to keep your business to yourself."

Bart snorted. "It don't matter you're out with your girlfriend. She's not gonna say anything." He looked around Gary through the window, raising his voice. "Are you, Rayne?"

The sound of my name from his sneering lips turned me to ice. I focused on my lap, frozen.

"Leave her out of this." Gary's voice sharpened.

"She's not *in* it. And if she knows what's good for her, she'll stay that way." Bart gestured to Andy. "Go get the stuff."

Andy strode to the black car. I heard a door open, then slam.

He returned carrying a small paper bag. Bart took it from him and pushed it into Gary's chest.

"The address and cost is inside. I want the money at my place in half an hour. Not a minute later." He swiveled and headed for his car, Andy following.

Gary slipped back inside the truck, stone-faced. He opened the paper bag and pulled out a white piece of paper. Stuffing the bag under his seat, he flicked on the overhead light.

Behind us the black car's engine throbbed. It pulled past the truck, did a U-turn in the middle of the street, and was gone.

I tried to swallow. "Gary—"

"Be quiet." He focused on the piece of paper.

Air gushed from his mouth. His head tilted back, the paper smacked against the seat. "The drop-off's fifteen minutes in the other direction from your house." Panic coated his voice.

"What does that mean? What's in the bag?"

He ran a hand across his mouth. "I figured I'd take you home first. But I can't. Not enough time."

I gawked at him, questions crowding my tongue.

Gary stared out the windshield, emotions moving over his face. Confusion … dread … anger … resolve. Abruptly, he sat up straight and shoved the truck into drive.

I dug my fingers into my jeans. "Where are we going?"

He hunched over the steering wheel, his jaw hard. "I have to deliver this, Rayne." The words pinched from him. "God forgive me, but I got to take you with me."

"What if you don't? What if you just *don't* do what they say?"

"You know what's in that bag, Rayne? Drugs. Want to know how much they're worth? *Two thousand* dollars. I have to get that money to Bart in half an hour, or they'll pay a visit to my grandmother. *Understand?*"

Two thousand dollars? No, I didn't understand. How could this possibly be true? He'd warned me months ago, but I'd wished it all away. Things like this just didn't happen in real life.

Gary turned left onto a busy street.

"What if you're caught?"

"I won't be."

"What if you *are*?"

"Shut up, Rayne!"

I pressed back in the seat, arms folded. Streetlights and cars surrounded us, but all I could see was a black, dead-end tunnel. If Gary kept doing these deliveries, one day he would be caught. He'd go to jail. I could see it now — he'd never say a word to the cops about Westrock, how they'd made him do this. Because if he did, they'd likely kill Grandma Donovon.

And if he didn't do these deliveries, he and his grandmother could both be killed.

No wonder the Westrock gang made him do their dirty work. They had nothing to lose if he was caught. And meanwhile they got to carry out their crimes without putting themselves on the line.

I pulled my arms across my chest. "Sorry. I'm just scared."

Gary hit the steering wheel with a fist. "I didn't want you ever to be a part of this."

"I know."

My eyes closed. What did this make me, an accomplice? If the police caught Gary tonight, would I go to jail too?

We drove the rest of the way in silence. My muscles turned to steel.

Gary turned into a rundown, dangerous neighborhood. Drugs and murders — that's what this area was known for. Just driving its streets, you were taking your life in your hands. Old cars lined the curb, porches sagging and paint peeling. Not one house had grass in the yard.

I slid lower in the seat. "How does someone who lives *here* afford two thousand dollars for drugs?"

"They're dealers. They sell the drugs for profit."

Gary picked up the piece of paper with trembling hands. The sight of his fear made my own body shake. "Two-oh-six." He slowed, peering at numbers on mailboxes, then pulled over at a dirty beige house.

He glanced up and down the street before sliding the paper bag from beneath the seat.

"Rayne, listen. I'm locking the doors. The minute I'm out of the truck, you slide behind the wheel. I'm going up to the house, make this deal, and come right back. But if anything happens to me, if you hear *anything*, I want you to drive away."

"I can't — "

"Just do what I say."

"But — "

Gary opened the door, hit the lock button, and got out. He shut the door and motioned to me furiously. "*Move.*"

I slid over.

As he walked around the front of the truck, I clutched the wheel, my heart pounding.

Gary reached the sidewalk — and an engine roared some distance behind me. Rap music burst in my ears. Gary swung toward the sound. I swiveled around in the seat.

A white sedan screeched to a stop behind the truck. In the rear-view mirror I saw a blur of motion. Two men jumped from the front seat doors, one holding something low at his side. They ran toward Gary. He froze.

The house's front door smashed open, and another man rushed out. Something black was clutched in his hand. "Hey!" He flew off the porch, veering toward the two men from the car. He raised his arm.

A gun. He had a *gun*.

Gary pivoted toward the truck. "Open the door!"

My body wouldn't move. Then my fingers were fumbling for the lock button. Where was it? Where *was* it? Blood pounded in my ears.

Gary yelled again, his face at the window.

The button clicked.

A blast ripped the night. My eyes snapped to the man who'd run from the house.

His face exploded.

I screamed. Jerked a look over my shoulder. One of the men from the car was lowering a shotgun.

Gary threw open the passenger door, still gripping the paper bag. He jumped inside. "Go, go!"

In the same second two more men dashed out of the house's gaping door, weapons raised. Gunfire rat-tatted. The man with the shotgun collapsed to the ground.

"Rayne!" Gary's face creased with terror. "Get *out* of here!"

I jammed the truck into drive and hit the accelerator.

29

We careened down the street and around the corner. I screamed the whole time. Twice I almost wrecked the truck.

Gary shoved the paper bag under the seat. The bag with drugs. The bag that had just caused the death of at least two people.

A few blocks away, Gary barked at me to pull to the curb. I jerked from behind the wheel, and he climbed over me to drive.

No one had followed.

Maybe they were all dead. Maybe they shot each other. Panicked as I was, I hoped it was true. I just didn't want any of them coming after us.

Five minutes passed before I could speak. We were back on a main road, lots of traffic. My heart had slowed to triple time.

"What happened?"

Gary shook his head. "Rival gangs."

Like one gang wasn't enough. I wiped my forehead. "What do we do now?"

"Take the stuff back to Bart. At least I didn't drop it on the street. If I returned without the money, without the drugs ..."

A shudder clawed at me. "What's he going to do?"

"I don't know."

When we got to Gary's house, Bart was standing on the lighted front porch. Waiting.

I gasped. *Grandma Donovon!* Gary yanked up the paper bag and leapt out of the truck. He strode toward Bart, arms pumping. Bart came down the steps.

"Somebody knew I was coming."

"Yeah, I got a call." Bart eyed the bag. "That better be full."

Gary's face purpled. He thrust the bag at Bart. "Nothing's lost. Nearly got killed, but what's that to you?"

Bart's eyes narrowed. He pulled his head back like a snake. "Wouldn't be taking that tone if I were you."

"Well, you're *not* me."

"If that's the way you want it." Bart shrieked a whistle. Immediately his two roommates stomped out their door, their figures barely visible in the dark. Bart gestured toward them. "You got somethin' else to say to us?"

I pressed my hand into the seat. The *coward.* Couldn't even take on Gary alone. He'd be squashed like a bug, and he knew it.

Bart's friends stalked across the lawn.

Gary held his ground. "You got what you wanted. Now get off my property."

"I didn't get what I wanted. I expected cash. You brought me the bag."

"What'd you think I'd do, stay there and get *shot*?"

A curtain edged back from Gary's front window. Grandma Donovon peeked out. Gary's head jerked toward her. She dropped the curtain and disappeared.

Bart's two grunt friends planted themselves a foot from Gary, one on each side. Both of them folded their arms and glared, daring him to keep it up.

"What I *know*" — Bart shoved his face into Gary's — "is that you'll do this job tonight, like I tell you to."

"No!" Gary slashed an arm through the air. "I'm not doing this *anymore* for you."

"You don't have a choice!"

"I just made one!"

Bart held his position, breathing like a bull. Slowly, his body relaxed. He eased back, gave a lazy shrug. "Tony." He raised his chin toward one of his friends. "Go get the old woman."

Tony swiveled toward the house.

"Stop!" Gary jumped him.

They crashed to the ground, fists and curses flying. Bart jumped back as the second guy dove on top of Gary.

"No!" I scrambled out of the truck. My heels hit a bump in the grass, and I went sprawling. I landed hard, the wind knocked out of me. All I could hear was the sound of punches and grunts.

Gary.

I flipped over and pushed myself to my feet. Tony and the other guy had Gary down, kicking and beating with all their might. I tottered over, screaming. Caught one by the arm and yanked. He threw me backward like I weighed nothing. I hit the ground on my side.

"Ungh." Air forced out my lungs. My teeth clattered together.

Behind me the smacks grew louder. They were going to kill Gary.

No. *No.* I managed to get up again, shaking and bruised. My legs turned to water. Vaguely I registered Bart pulling Grandma Donovon out of the house. White-faced, she pleaded for them to stop.

Bart raised a hand. "Hold it."

Tony and the other guy backed off, chests heaving.

"Gary!" I flailed over to him and dropped to the grass, sobbing. "Garyyyyy." Blood covered his face, oozing from his nose and mouth. He barely moved.

Bart sauntered over like he was waiting for a bus. He sneered down at Gary and sniffed.

"I'm going to be *extra nice* and give you some time to think about your attitude." He motioned to his two friends. "Let's go."

As they walked away, Bart threw final words over his shoulder. "We'll be back."

PART 11
Monday 2009

30

Franklin's plane took off from Phoenix on time.

He sat in an aisle seat near the back, his long legs cramped, and his brain crackling with anticipation. He'd waited for this chance for so long. But too many things could go wrong.

Stupid Jerry. Couldn't do a job right. Franklin should have known better than to trust the man.

At Franklin's gate at the airport, a TV mounted from the ceiling had been turned to CNN. Four times as he waited he'd seen footage of Rayne's accident and Shaley leaping from her limo, screaming.

Shaley. His daughter. He *knew* that, even though Rayne had never told him she was pregnant. The last time he saw her, she couldn't have known yet, he'd bet on that. August 30, 1992. A day he would never forget.

Franklin wondered how far the hospital was from the Denver airport.

He closed his eyes, chin lowered toward his chest. He needed a thorough plan, but it wouldn't come. He needed to get there first, see the layout and the odds against him.

Sometimes you needed to case the situation before deciding what to do.

Sloppiness is what got him caught for the armed robbery. He'd held up a convenience store at night, never thinking about the security cameras. Dumb, dumb.

The stewardess came around, taking drink orders and offering a bag of peanuts. Franklin crunched his snack, barely tasting it. His thoughts whirled, imagining scenarios. If he did this thing wrong, his life could end today. Just like Jerry's.

Franklin tipped up the bag of peanuts and shook the last ones into his mouth. He wadded the crackly container in his palm.

No. Failure was not an option. He *would* reach his goal. By the end of this day, he would find a way into the hospital room of Rayne O'Connor.

31

W e'll be back ..."
    Mom's voice faded, and her eyelids fluttered. In my
head pulsed the bloody picture of Gary on the ground, beaten and
near senseless. I held Mom's hand, tears running down my face. I
couldn't begin to imagine what she had gone through. To watch
someone you love being hurt like that. To not be able to do anything about it.

How had that Gary become a criminal?

"I'm sorry," Mom whispered. "All of a sudden I'm so tired." She
swallowed.

"It's probably the medication." Half an hour ago a nurse had
been in to bring her two more pills.

I picked up Mom's water glass and held the straw to her lips. She
took a long drink.

With a sad smile, I set the glass down. "You want to sleep for
awhile?"

Her mouth twisted. "Yeah. But I know you want to hear the end.
I'll finish, then rest."

Our eyes locked, and I knew she meant more than simply take
a nap. After seventeen years, telling the story she'd bottled up for
so long had drained her. She wanted to be done with it. I had the
fleeting thought that once she finished, she'd never want to mention my father's name again.

And why would I want to hear it? Now I just wanted him sent

back to prison. Maybe he and Cat would end up in the same cell. Wouldn't they have a great time.

My eyes filled with fresh tears.

"What is it, Shaley?"

"Nothing." I blinked hard. "Just ... tell me the rest. I have to know."

Mom put her hand on my knee. "Like I said, people can change a lot in seventeen years."

But how? What happened then that made my father go bad?

"Did Bart and his friends come back?" I asked.

The pained look returned to Mom's eyes. She rubbed the bump on her head. "It was way more than just 'coming back'..."

PART 12
Rayne 1992

32

G ary." I leaned over him, my tears falling on his bloodied shirt. "Can you hear me?"

Grandma Donovon sank to her knees on his other side. She slipped a hand beneath his head and cradled it. "Gary." Even though she was crying too, her voice was amazingly calm. "You need to get up. We've got to get you out of here."

Rage exploded within me. I wanted to run after Bart and tear his eyes out. "Shouldn't we call the cops?" I demanded. Who cared about Bart's threats? I'd have stepped in front of a train at that moment if it meant seeing Bart and his lowlife friends behind bars.

Grandma Donovon gave me a hard look. "You see my grandson? This is what happens when you stand up to these people."

Gary groaned. "Rayne?" His eyes were still closed, his voice breathy.

My heart leapt. "I'm here."

"Help me up."

I threw a terrified look at Grandma Donovon. She couldn't really mean he should move. What if he had broken bones? What if moving him injured him more?

She nodded. "It's our only choice. Or they'll kill him."

That's the first time in my life I remember sincerely praying for God's help. I begged him to let the two of us get Gary out of there. Then slowly, carefully, we supported Gary as he sat up and struggled to his feet. He was badly bruised and sore, but nothing seemed broken. We got him in the passenger seat of the truck. I

172 ～◯ Brandilyn Collins and Amberly Collins

climbed into the driver's seat and scooted to the middle. Grandma Donovon drove.

I gave her directions to my house.

When we pulled into the driveway my mom was still gone. She'd made plans to go out with friends that night. Grandma Donovon and I eased Gary out of the truck and up our front porch. I unlocked the door, and we walked him inside and to the couch.

"I need clean cloths and warm water." Grandma Donovon rolled up the sleeves of her casual shirt.

When I brought the large pan of water and washcloths, she began cleaning off the blood. Then she probed his face, neck, ribs, and arms with efficient, gentle fingers. I gave her a questioning look.

"Used to be a nurse." She sat back on her haunches, gazing at Gary with glistening eyes. "Before my heart condition made me have to quit."

"I'm sorry." Gary moved his head and winced. "Grandma, I don't ... I should have just done what they said."

"And go to jail for *their* crimes?"

Gary's eyes opened. He looked at her in dull surprise.

She snorted. "Don't think I don't know what you've been doing. Thinking you were protecting me. But it's not going to happen again. *No more.*"

Gary's eyes slipped shut. "We can't go back home."

The phone rang. I ignored it.

"That's not your fault." Grandma Donovon wiped her brow. The edges of her rolled-up sleeves were wet.

In the kitchen the phone kept ringing. I made a face at it. After six rings it cut off, sat silent a few seconds, then started ringing again.

"We'll have to move." Gary swallowed. "I have to get our stuff out of there somehow ..."

Three rings.

A startling thought rattled through my brain.

Four.

Tingles started up my spine. In a half daze I walked to the kitchen's door and stared at the phone, as if it would tell me who was calling. But somehow I knew.

My head whipped back toward Gary and his grandmother. She was leaning down close to him, talking.

Our answering machine kicked on. I listened to my mother's voice invite the caller to leave a message. My body tensed.

"We *let* you leave, you know." The hated voice came through the recorder. Low, menacing. Grandma Donovon cut off mid-sentence. Gary's hand jerked.

"I got to go out tonight and take care of some business, Gary. Come see me tomorrow."

Click. The answering machine fell silent.

Grandma Donovon, Gary, and I looked at each other.

My mind is vague about the rest of that evening. I felt too wrung out to listen with a clear head as Gary and his grandmother talked. What could they do? Going to the police — *if* they connected with one that wasn't on the take with Bart — would mean waiting for weeks or even months to testify against Westrock. By that time they'd be dead. Going home meant putting themselves under Bart's thumb again. It would only be a matter of time before Gary took the fall for one of their drug runs.

One unspoken answer hung in the air. The more they talked, the heavier it hovered over our heads and weighed our shoulders.

Around midnight Mom came home. We told her everything — we had no choice. Mom stared at Gary, appalled, then ran around fixing him food, doing anything she could to make him comfortable. But a moment came when she edged me aside and gave me a look that seared my heart. An accusing expression that said *this has been going on with Gary for months, and you've said nothing? Don't you see the danger you've put us in?*

Gary, by now sitting up on the couch, saw the unspoken exchange. The horrible knowledge of what he must do flattened his face.

174 ◦ Brandilyn Collins and Amberly Collins

He couldn't be with me anymore.

No. My stomach flipped over. There would be another way—

The phone rang. It was Bart.

"Look forward to seeing you tomorrow, Gary."

Click.

Mom's eyes lasered mine. There wasn't a single thing I could say in response.

We all needed sleep. Grandma Donovon was given our spare bedroom. Gary would stay on the couch. I drifted into my room, numb and sick to the core. Somehow I drifted off.

Until a pounding rattled my door at four o'clock in the morning.

33

I jolted awake, heart banging. Before I knew it I'd jumped from bed and thrown back the door.

Gary swayed on his feet in the hall.

I gasped.

He jammed his forearm against the wall and leaned into it. His mouth hung open, air stuttering down his throat and a wild glaze in his eyes. "Rayne." His mouth quivered.

My legs started to shake. Never had I seen Gary cry. "What?"

His eyes closed. "The house. It's burned down."

"What? What house?"

"My ... grandma's house. They burned it."

I stared at him. Had he gone out of his mind?

Gary dragged his eyes open. He wouldn't look at me. "I drove over there ... Wanted to sneak in ... get a few things. It's gone, Rayne. Everything's gone."

Footsteps sounded from the guestroom. Grandma Donovon appeared in her doorway, still in her clothes. "What's going on?"

Another door clicked. Mom scurried into the hall, a frightened look on her face.

"Grandma." Gary pushed up straight. His face twisted with sick determination. "Get in the truck. We're leaving."

"What? We—"

"Get. In. The truck." He turned to her, bruised hands on his hips. "We have to go. We have to get out of town. Now."

"Why?"

"Our house is burned to the ground. We've got nothing left but our lives. And I'm not letting them take yours."

Grandma Donovon's eyes rounded. "My house is *gone*?"

Gary nodded.

"Ohhh!" She swooned. Mom ran to her.

Gary looked back to me. "Rayne —" His voice pinched off. He held up a hand, struggling to speak. "If Bart ever calls you again, tell him exactly this: 'After you burned down Gary's house, he and his grandmother left the state. He's never coming back. And nobody's going to the police.' You tell him that, and he'll leave you alone."

"Gary, *no*!" I reached for him, my whole world dropping away. "You can't go!"

He stepped back and held up both hands, palms out, as if to protect himself from me. But his eyes told the truth. If he faltered now, if he hesitated one little bit, he'd lose his resolve — and stay.

And the four of us would never be safe.

"Grandma." His gaze held mine. I thought I would die. "Get in the truck."

She threw a shocked look at me and started down the hall.

"Gary —" I wanted to scream that he'd change his mind in a day or two. He'd come back. Somehow, some way, we'd work this out ...

But my heart caught in my throat, and my knees turned to water.

"Rayne." His voice caught. "I love you."

He turned away and walked down the hall.

A cry wrenched from me. Gary's back stiffened. For a second he slowed. Then he pushed himself forward once more.

I gripped the doorway, deep sobs punching out of my mouth. This couldn't be happening. None of it was real.

Gary disappeared around the corner.

My legs gave way. I sank to my knees on the carpet.

The front door opened and closed.

Only then did I realize the sound I heard from our driveway. The engine of his truck, already running.

No!

Sudden energy surged through me. I shoved to my feet and pounded down the hall. Mom yelled at me to stop, but I paid no attention. I careened around the corner, flung myself through the front door and out on the porch.

"Garyyyy!"

He'd just finished backing out of the driveway. The truck surged forward.

My last view of Gary Donovon was through the driver's window. I glimpsed his steel profile, every finger clenched around the wheel as though any minute his brittle body would break.

Then he was gone.

PART 13
Monday 2009

34

I stared at Mom in shock. Her face twisted in pain — more from the memories, I thought, than from her injuries.

"That's *it*?" I leaned toward her. "He just ... disappeared — like *that*?"

She nodded then turned her head toward the window. The trail of a tear glistened on her temple.

"Did he ever call you?"

"No."

"What about Bart? Did he call you, demanding to know where Gary went?"

"Yeah, for months. But I truly didn't know. Gary proved right about that. As long as Bart could sense I wasn't lying, there was no point in coming after me."

I sat back, rubbing my forehead. "But it's still so hard to believe. How could Gary just leave you like that?"

"He wanted to protect me, Shaley."

Yeah, or maybe he started robbing stores right away. "He could have called. He could have at least told you where he'd gone."

Mom shifted her focus back to me. She looked so very tired. "I kept thinking he would. Day after day I kept believing he'd show up on my doorstep one night. But ... nothing."

"He loved you. *How* could he leave?"

"I think he loved me enough to leave. And he had to protect his grandmother. Those gang members — they never would have left the three of us alone if he'd stayed in the area. He had to get far away, far enough that they'd know he wouldn't be a threat to them."

"But why didn't he call?"

She shook her head. "I think he ... couldn't. If he called, if he heard my voice, it might be too much for him to take, and he'd come back."

"That doesn't make sense."

"It's the only sense I can make of it. I *know* he loved me. I know he didn't want to go. Besides, there were the roses. The first came a week after he'd left. Then, like clockwork, they arrived twice a month. Always with the same message as before: *You are a white rose to me. I love you. Gary.*"

I thought of what she'd said — that they stopped coming eight years ago. Only then did I realize what that meant. "That means he sent them for *nine years* after he left."

"Yeah."

I frowned. "You'd be twenty-five by then. I was eight. I don't remember anything about white roses."

"They came to my mom's house, Shaley. That's the only address he knew. She would call and let me know. She'd read me the words on the card. Then she would keep the rose until it wilted."

"Why didn't you bring them home?" We lived near my grandmother until her death from breast cancer when I was nine.

Mom lowered her gaze. "I didn't want you asking questions."

What? "I *was* asking questions. I've been asking you about my father for as long as I can remember."

"Exactly. It was easier to tell you I didn't know where he was. That was the truth. How to explain the flowers to you, how to tell an eight year old the story I've just told you?"

I looked away, betrayal sloshing around inside me. To think all those years when I was little, she'd still had a tie to my father. A long-distance tie, but it was *something*. She told me *nothing*. How unfair, that I couldn't at least have known what she knew — he was out there somewhere, thinking about us.

I closed my eyes, fighting the emotion. I didn't want to go there now. "Did you ever call the florist that delivered them? Try to find out from them where he was?" I'd done the same thing just a few days ago, after I received my own white rose ...

"He paid by credit card and ordered over the phone. They wouldn't give me his address."

"And then they just stopped coming?"

"Yes." Mom fingered the top of her covers. "I didn't even notice for a couple months. By then, after so many years, I was busy with you and the band. I'd moved on. When I realized it, I told myself he'd found someone else." Her mouth curled in a bitter smile. "It was easier to think that than believe something had happened to him." She sighed. "Now I know something did. Prison."

My heart panged. "Are you surprised he did that?"

She focused across the room. "Those gang members taught him crime, Shaley. Not that he wanted to do those drug runs. But once he ran away, and he and his grandmother had to build a new life ... maybe he thought back to all the thousands of dollars he watched them rake in, selling drugs. Maybe he figured there were easier ways to make money than earn it."

"But he wasn't caught selling drugs."

"Doesn't mean he didn't do it. Who knows how many crimes he committed before he was caught?"

My gaze fell to the floor. She was right—who knew? If Jerry hadn't whispered in my ear, we wouldn't even know my father had sent him to us.

May 1993—my birth month. I counted back nine months from then. "When he left you didn't know you were pregnant."

Mom's face softened. "No. I found out about a month later."

One month. "What if you had known? If you'd told him—maybe he never would have gone."

"Don't think about that." Mom's voice flattened. "I wished the same thing—if only the timing would have been one month different. But that would have made things worse. He *had* to leave. If he'd stayed because of you, who knows what would have happened to him?"

But *one month* ... My lifetime of questions for a single month.

"Yeah. I guess."

We'd never talked much about her pregnancy with me. Except that she'd told me not to make the same mistake. It wasn't a good thing to do — sleeping with boyfriends. And I hadn't.

The light in Mom's eyes dimmed, exhaustion creeping over her face. Too many memories and too much pain. "Think I'll take a nap now."

"Okay." I squeezed her hand and stood.

Mom lolled her head to one side and immediately drifted to sleep.

I stood in the middle of the room, feeling lost and purposeless. All the years I'd begged to hear my father's story. Now I had. But I wasn't satisfied. It brought only more questions.

Why had he never called Mom? Why had he turned to crime?

Deep disappointment churned within me, thickening into bitterness. So what if my father had once loved Mom? He'd turned out to be a rat. Left her in the dust. Held up a store and gone to prison. Then even sent a murderer to kill people on our tour and try to kidnap me.

Why?

Jealousy. Had to be. Rayne O'Connor became famous while he'd gone nowhere. I could just imagine him seeing her on TV in jail, gritting his teeth. Did he brag to all the prisoners that he used to date her?

Or maybe he wanted to kidnap me for ransom. Figured he'd take Mom for all the money he could.

My shoulders slumped. The tiredness I'd been holding back washed over me. I walked over to my bed and lay down on top of the covers.

Tears bit my eyes. I felt lonely and worn out, and I hated this hospital room. I just wanted to go *home*.

Turning on my side, I curled into a ball. Sleep pulled at me. I closed my eyes and gave in to it . . .

The next thing I knew my cell phone was ringing me awake.

35

Franklin's plane landed in Denver at five thirty. With no baggage to worry about, he was up the ramp and out of the airport in five minutes.

Outside, the air felt hot but nothing like Phoenix. The lanes teemed with cars, doors slamming, people scurrying with luggage. Franklin looked around, getting his bearings. He spotted the area for taxis and walked over.

A Middle Eastern cabbie waved him to a car, and Franklin slid into the back seat. His hand reached for his pocket, feeling the bulk of his cell phone.

"Where are you going, sir?" The dark-eyed man surveyed him through the rearview mirror.

"St. Joseph's Hospital."

"No problem. I have you there fast."

"Can you make a stop first?"

"Where?"

Franklin told him. "I won't be long. I know what I want."

On the plane Franklin had thought it over. He couldn't just walk into this wild plan of his without backup.

The cabbie eyed him. "Whatever you say."

He hit the accelerator and darted out into traffic.

36

Like a drugged person, I reached toward the table where my cell phone lay. My heavy eyes checked the incoming ID. With a sigh, I hit *send*. "Hi, Ross."

"Hi. Sounds like you were sleeping."

Yeah, and he didn't sound a bit sorry about waking me. "What's up?"

"Your mom sleeping too?"

I raised myself up, squinting at her. Let my head fall back to the pillow. "Yeah, she's out. The pills and pain finally got to her."

"When she wakes up, tell her I called. I booked a charter flight for the band tomorrow afternoon. Couldn't get one today."

"Okay."

"Also, Mick's going to show up soon to relieve Wendell at his post outside your door."

"Uh-huh." Man, my head felt dull.

The line fell silent.

"That's it," Ross said. "You can go back to sleep now."

"'Kay. Thanks."

I clicked off the line and closed my eyes. In two seconds the phone rang again.

Now what did Ross want? With a frustrated growl I punched on the call. "Hel-*lo*."

"Hi. Shaley?"

Detective Myner's voice. I sat up.

"Hi. Sorry. I thought you were someone else."

"No problem." He hesitated. "Perhaps I should speak to your mom."

"She's asleep."

"Oh. In that case you need to know something has come up."

He sounded so serious. "Okay."

"In searching for Franklin Borden, one of my men checked with the airlines to see if anyone using that name had taken a flight out of Phoenix. We thought it was a long shot, but we got a hit. Borden caught a flight some time after three o'clock. Unfortunately, we learned this too late to intercept him upon his arrival."

An alarm buzzed in my head. I shot a protective glance at my mom. Still asleep. "Where'd he go?"

The detective cleared his throat. "Denver."

Denver. My mouth sagged open. "You mean he's *here*? *Now*?"

"He landed about thirty-five minutes ago. We've got his photo and are checking the airport, but we're probably too late. He's likely to have seen television news stories about your mom's accident, which unfortunately have named her current location. Our guess is he's headed for the hospital."

My stomach turned to ice.

"Shaley, we're sending officers there right now. We're going to put one outside your room, and others will be checking entrances to the hospital, plus every floor. It's a big place. But I want you to believe me when I say we're going to stop this guy."

My mind whirled. I found myself standing. Couldn't even remember getting off the bed. "Yeah. Sure. Okay."

"You all right? An officer will be at your door in just a few minutes."

"I ... I'm fine." My heart tripped into a hard beat.

"Don't leave your room. And have your phone close by. I'll keep you posted."

"Th-thanks."

I clicked off the call and stared at nothing. My brain wouldn't focus.

Mom. I threw her another glance, praying she'd sleep through this. Let her wake up to hear Franklin Borden had been caught, that we were safe. That it was *over.*

I jerked toward the door to tell Wendell.

37

Franklin peered through the taxi windshield as it drove up the long entryway to the hospital. Around him loomed a huge building shaped like a squared U. The main section lay directly ahead, with a wing running down each side of the road. In front of the main entrance was a circular drive for dropping off and picking up passengers.

The purchase Franklin had made sat in a box on the seat beside him. Best way to carry it, he figured. Not likely anyone would question what was inside.

As the taxi neared the circular section, Franklin spotted a crowd of people near the main hospital door. His eyes narrowed. He saw reporters, cameramen, and lots of fans. Some carried signs that said "Get well soon, Rayne."

He pressed back against the seat. Not good. He didn't want his face picked up on some camera.

The driver clucked his tongue. "It's that rock singer. You know the one?"

"Yeah." Franklin kept his voice even. "Drive around the circle and go back down a ways."

"Whatever you say, sir." The cabbie did as he was asked, then pulled over. "This okay?"

"Fine." Franklin took out his wallet and paid the man. "Keep the change." He lifted the box off the seat and got out.

As the taxi drove off, Franklin turned back to survey the scene in front of the hospital. He'd have to find another way in. He looked around, gauging the buildings.

Franklin spied a door and started toward it, then halted. Just getting inside wasn't good enough. Nobody at the information desk was going to give him the room number for Rayne O'Connor.

Sticking his tongue beneath his upper lip, he gazed at the main entrance once more. Somebody in that crowd might have inside information. Someone with a relative who worked in the hospital ...

His focus moved to the TV cameras. For the moment none of them were running.

He did have a second option. It was the main reason he'd bought a cell phone in the first place.

Maybe he'd use it. Maybe not.

Raising his chin, Franklin set out down the long stretch of pavement to join the crowd of Rayne O'Connor fans.

38

Within five minutes of Detective Myner's phone call, just like he'd promised, a hard-faced Denver policeman had stationed himself outside Mom's door. He had that cop look, just by the way he moved. He took up position on the right, Wendell on the left. No way anyone was getting through those two.

"I was in the area, so I got here quickly," the officer told me as I talked to them in the hall. His name tag read *Tripton*. "Back-ups are on their way."

His radio crackled quietly with voices I could barely hear. He must have turned down the volume so it wouldn't disturb the whole hospital wing.

Wendell reached for his phone. I caught his arm. "What are you doing?"

"Calling Ross. He should know."

"No, Wendell! Please." I didn't want Ross rushing over. Didn't want to see the I-told-you-so expression on his face. Part of me knew I misjudged him — at a time like this, Ross wouldn't blame me. Maybe it was just my own guilt. Still, I didn't want him around.

"What's he going to do?" I gestured toward the cop. "It's not like we don't have enough help here."

Wendell hesitated.

"Besides, Mick's coming anytime now to take your place. Let him make the decision."

And when Mick got here, I'd convince *him* not to make the call.

Wendell exchanged a look with the officer and put his phone away. "Teenagers."

"Tell me about it. I got two of 'em."

I shook back my hair and retreated inside. Fingers jammed to my temples, I paced the room.

How long would this take? What if they didn't catch Franklin Borden? Maybe he wasn't even at the hospital. For all we knew he'd flown here to see relatives.

Yeah right. Some coincidence.

My mouth hardened. When they caught the man, *I* planned to pay him a visit. When they questioned him, I'd be there. Watching through one of those one-way mirrors, like I'd watched the San Jose police question Cat.

No, forget that. Whatever it took, I'd be *in* the room with the man. I had a few questions for Franklin Borden myself.

In her bed, Mom stirred. I tiptoed over, heart in my throat. Her eyes blinked half open. "Shaley." Her voice slurred. "What time is it?"

"Time for you to go back to sleep," I whispered.

Her eyelids fluttered, then closed.

I curled my fingers into fists and watched her breathe.

39

Keeping his back to the cameras, Franklin circulated through the group of fans. He held the box down by his side. In five minutes he'd pulled the information he needed from a fresh-faced twenty-something blonde who couldn't gush enough about how much she loved Rayne's music. Rayne O'Connor was on the third floor, she told him. She knew somebody who knew somebody whose mom was a nurse in the hospital. Had actually been in the rock star's room.

"Can you *imagine*?" She spread her black-painted fingernails across her chest.

Franklin gave her a tight smile. "You try going up there to see her?"

The young woman tsked through her teeth. "Yeah, right. She's got a private bodyguard posted outside that room."

"Oh?"

"Yup. 'Round the clock."

Franklin kept a poker face. *Bodyguard at the door.* Not surprising.

"Her daughter's with her too," the young woman added. "Shaley."

"You sure?"

"Yeah. She slept there." The young woman focused over his shoulder, as if something had caught her attention. "Wouldn't leave her mom."

"Have you —"

"Hey, look at that." Her eyebrows raised.

He looked around — and stilled. Five police cars were coming down the entrance road. They pulled over to the curb some distance away, one after the other, and cut their engines.

"Maybe something's wrong with Rayne." The young woman's voice edged with worry.

Franklin gripped the bag, his thoughts swirling. He arrives … and the police show up. Did they know he was here?

Why would they even be paying attention to him? Unless they knew he was connected to Jerry Brand.

But the news stories had said nothing about the police looking for him. Nothing about connecting him to Brand.

Maybe the police had kept it quiet so he wouldn't be alerted. That had to be it. Hard to believe this was a coincidence.

Franklin gritted his teeth. They'd arrest him. Question him in some dim little room. *We know you sent Brand to the Rayne tour. How much did you pay him to kill those two people? To kidnap Shaley?*

A buzz spread through the crowd as people nudged each other and pointed to the policemen approaching, now about twenty feet away. The area exploded with action. Every reporter around rushed the officers, yelling questions. TV cameras switched on.

"Why are you here?" one fan called out. "Is it Rayne?"

The policemen never even slowed.

Keeping his head down, Franklin eased toward the nearest hospital door and slipped inside.

A minute. He had no more time than that. If they were looking for him — and he knew they were — every officer would be carrying a copy of his picture.

Shaley was here. He couldn't have asked for better news.

He forced himself to walk at a normal pace, chin up. Like he had nothing to hide. But his eyes cut right and left.

Franklin spotted signs for the elevators. Too much of a gamble to take one. Where else to go?

He turned down a long corridor, plans revving in his brain. The cops would focus their search on men in street clothes. If he could get to the laundry area of the hospital, locate where they kept uniforms for new employees...

An exit sign for a stairwell appeared some distance away. Franklin strode for the door and stepped through. He pounded down the stairs to the sub-ground levels. Somewhere in the guts of the hospital, he'd find what he needed.

40

Eternal minutes ticked by. I paced the room, arms tight across my chest. Again and again I sidled over to the window, peering through half-closed blinds. I saw nothing unusual on the road below me. Were more policemen arriving? There were probably all coming in the front door.

I'd turned my cell phone to vibrate and placed it on the floor near the suitcases. If it went off, I'd hear it buzz against the hard surface.

Mom slept on.

An orderly had brought her dinner. It sat on the rolling table by my bed, food still covered. The smell of meatloaf wafted from the tray.

The clock read 6:30. A mere twenty-four hours ago Mom and I had been huddled in the manager's office of our San Jose hotel. Jerry had just been shot by police. Bruce was dead. I'd been kidnapped and rescued. *Twenty-four hours.* It seemed like a lifetime. And was it only one day we'd been cooped up in this hospital room?

Please, God, help them find my father. Bring an end to this.

My throat felt like a desert. I stole a drink from Mom's glass.

For all the years I'd longed to know the truth about my father, I'd now give anything to return to that ignorance. At least then I had hope. Now the only hope I had about Gary Donovon, a.k.a. Franklin Borden, was that he'd be caught. I wanted him behind bars for the rest of his life for what he'd done. Jerry Brand may have pulled the trigger that killed Tom and Bruce, but my father had sent him here.

And just what would have happened to *me* if the police and Wendell hadn't found me when they did?

A light knock sounded on the door. I scurried to answer it.

Mick towered over me in the hall, his expression grim. "Just wanted you to know we've changed shifts out here." He kept his voice low.

I glanced from him to the policeman. "Okay. Thanks."

"You need anything?"

"No. Mom's asleep."

"Good." He gave me a tight smile.

I looked to the officer. "Are other policemen here now?"

He nodded. "We got people all over this hospital, Miss O'Connor."

My heart turned over. The answer was supposed to comfort me, but it sounded terrifying. To think so many police were needed ...

"Okay." My voice pinched. "Thanks."

I shut the door and leaned against it, trembling.

Five more minutes passed. I wandered the room, sat down on my bed, got up again.

I turned on the TV, muting the sound. Flipped through cable channels, searching for news. One station spritzed onto a scene of a reporter in front of an excited crowd. People waved signs — "We love you, Rayne." "Get well soon, Rayne."

My eyes locked to the screen. Was that the front of the hospital? Yesterday, we'd come in through the emergency room entrance.

"In the last fifteen minutes we've seen about a dozen policemen arrive," the reporter said. "They wouldn't tell us why they're here, but it appears to have something to do with Rayne O'Connor. Our last word as to the singer's condition is that she's stable, although in a lot of pain. Reports are that her daughter, Shaley, is with her."

Behind the reporter a lanky figure darted from the crowd toward the hospital's entrance. A man wearing jeans and a white

T-shirt, with a bushy brown afro and beard. He carried a backpack. The different shirt and disguise didn't fool me for a minute.

Cat.

Rage shot through me. Forgetting everything but this, I swiveled toward the door. Nobody would stop me this time. I would catch that horrible man myself—

A loud *burr* went off behind me. My cell phone, vibrating against the floor. *Cat, calling me again.* What did he have now, a new picture to blackmail me with?

I dashed back for the phone. All I'd have to do is keep him on the line long enough for the police to get him ...

I snatched the cell off the floor and hit the *send* button.

41

The orderly uniform wasn't good enough.

Franklin had snuck into a supply room, found a uniform, and put it on. But he couldn't locate the security badges that hung around the orderly's necks. And even if he did, the plastic area would be empty; no photo, no name. Any officer close enough to him would notice.

But if an officer got close, it would be too late for him anyway. His face was the bigger problem.

Clutching his box, he slunk up multiple flights of stairs and stepped onto the third floor.

One good thing about the bodyguard protecting Rayne and Shaley—the man's presence outside a door would signal Rayne's room.

Franklin passed multiple patient rooms, some with doors closed, others open. He glanced inside the open ones as he went by. Three looked empty.

Up ahead was a corner. He slowed, cocking his head to listen. Voices filtered around the wall, sounding some distance away. He edged close and leaned forward until one eye cleared to see.

Another corridor of rooms. Some thirty feet down sat a nurse's station. Two policemen talked nearby.

Long, long down the hall, past the nurse's station and almost to the end, two men stood at attention on either side of a door. One in plainclothes. The other in a cop's uniform.

Rayne's room.

Franklin jerked his head back. His chest turned to lead. *Two men guarding the room.* One a police officer. How was he going to get inside?

Voices sounded from another connecting hallway behind him. Franklin glanced right and left. He spotted a door to a room he remembered as empty. He darted toward it, jumped inside, and pulled the door shut.

Seconds later, the voices passed by.

Franklin's shoulders relaxed. He turned and set the box on the nearest bed. With narrowed eyes he focused out the window. He looked out on a side street. No sign of cops.

He pulled his cell phone from his pocket.

Franklin had memorized the number months ago, when Jerry had given it to him over the phone. He hadn't wanted to use it today. Too many risks involved. He'd be better at persuading in person. But now he had no choice.

Staring at the cell, Franklin took a deep breath — and punched in the number.

42

"W hat do you want, Cat?" I spat into the phone as I hurried to the door.

Silence. I threw a glance over my shoulder at Mom. Still sleeping. "Hello?"

"Shaley." A man's voice. Not Cat's.

My feet slowed for a second, then picked up speed again. "Whoever you are, I can't talk right n — "

"Wait, don't hang up! I have to talk to you."

"Who is this?" I thrust my hand toward the door handle.

"Franklin Borden."

I slammed to a halt. All I could do was stare at the door, my hand hanging in the air. All my rage at Cat shifted toward this loser of a father. But the rage went far deeper, darker.

"Shaley?"

"Mom's sleeping. What do you want?" The words fell hard and accusing. My fingers dug into the phone.

"I wanted to talk to *you*. You know who I am?"

Both my knees went weak. I stumbled to the bed and sat down. Rational thought pushed into my brain. *Get him to tell you where he is so you can tell the police!* But every wretched hope I'd ever had of talking to this man clogged in my throat. "I know you left my mother seventeen years ago and never looked back."

"I didn't want to go, Shaley."

"Then why did you?"

"Has your mom told you the whole story?"

I couldn't believe this. I was talking to the man who left my mother. Who left *me*.

"You could have called. You could have told her where you were."

"I . . . sent her flowers."

I snorted. "Yeah, and then they stopped — when you went to prison."

"Look. There's so much to say. This isn't the way I'd hoped this conversation would go."

"What did you expect? Like you could just call me after all these years?"

"Listen." He spoke pleadingly. "I didn't even know you existed until four years ago. Not until your mom's band became famous and she was on TV. I saw an interview with her and heard her mention a daughter turning twelve that month. I was shocked. I didn't know."

Bitterness sizzled in my veins. "You were in prison then."

"True. And because of that there was no way I could even try to reach Rayne."

"You were there because you held up a store. With a gun."

"I —"

"Doesn't sound like a person I'd *want* to be my father."

"Shaley." His voice caught. "I was wrong. An idiot. My grandmother had recently died, I'd lost my job. Almost lost my soul. It was a stupid, stupid move. If I'd even thought about it another second, I never would have done it."

Liar.

Behind me, I heard Mom stir. I hunched over, covering my mouth with a hand. "Well, you should have taken that second."

"I know. I'm sorry I let you down. It's the last thing I'd ever want to do."

My teeth clenched. "You let me down by never being there for me in the first place."

"Please. I'm not a bad person. I've just made mistakes."

"*Mistakes?* A mistake is a wrong answer on a math test. A good person doesn't walk into a store and stick a gun in some innocent clerk's face."

"I get why you feel that way. But that's behind me now. I served my time. Now I'm asking you for forgiveness."

Yeah, right. "Why should I give it?"

He sighed. "You're young. Some day you're going to learn people aren't black or white. We're all shades of gray. Even a good person can make a mistake. I'm asking you not to judge until I can show you who I really am now."

"I know who you are," I hissed. "You're the one who sent Jerry Brand here. He killed two people and tried to kidnap me."

"I didn't know he'd do that! I thought I could trust him."

"Uh-huh."

"I just wanted him to get close to you and your mother so he could tell me about you. I wanted to know what your life's like, who your friends are. I just wanted to *know* about my daugh — "

"He *killed* two people!"

"I don't know why he did that. He went crazy. He was never like that when I knew him."

"He was *in jail* with you."

"But he'd served his time, and he said he just wanted to build a new life. I had no idea what he would do. I'd never want to hurt you like that. Never."

My eyes squeezed shut. I so wished I could believe the words. "What do you want from me?"

"I want to see you. To see your mom. I've dreamed of that for years."

Something new in his tone cut right through me. He sounded so sincere. I couldn't think of a thing to say. The little girl inside me who'd longed for a father *wanted* to believe. That little girl balanced on an ocean cliff, wanting to let go and fall into his words. Let his story wash away the pain . . .

Your father sent me.

I thought of Mom, the band members. Ross. So many people's safety depended on this man being found. And now I was talking to him on the phone.

My heart leapt again with yearning for my father. How could I possibly turn him in to the police? I could at least warn him the police were looking for him. If he left Denver now, maybe they wouldn't find him ...

And then what, Shaley? Leave him on the loose to come after you again?

My eyes squeezed shut. I had to face reality. Here I was talking to my father for the first time in my life — but I couldn't allow myself to believe his lies.

Do it, Shaley. Do what you have to do.

I thrust back my shoulders. "Where are you?"

"Will you see me?"

An evasive answer. I went cold. He must be close.

"What does that mean? How could I see you in Phoenix?"

"Don't play dumb, Shaley. You know I'm in Denver. The police know."

And one's standing outside my door.

"Why did you come here?"

"I had to see you. I had to know if Rayne's all right. I saw the news on TV of her accident. And when I heard what Jerry did, I was so mad. I couldn't believe it ..."

That tone again. I wanted to lose myself in it. Maybe he really did care.

He's lying and you know it.

But what if he wasn't?

Did I want this man — my *father* — surrounded by policemen with guns pointed at him? The father I'd never even met? The police had done the same to Jerry. And Jerry was *dead*.

Tears burned my eyes. Again I thought of Mom and the band members. How could I leave them in danger? How could I leave myself in danger?

"You really want to see me?" My voice almost cracked.

"Yes. More than anything."

"Then you have to tell me where you are."

He hesitated. "I'm at the hospital."

His answer knocked the wind out of me. "Oh." Somehow I managed to sound calm. "I'm at the hospital too."

"Really?" Excitement tinged his voice. "Didn't know that. Can you meet me somewhere?"

Any hope left inside me died. Now I could prove he was lying. Even the reporters knew I was here at the hospital. He had to know that too.

My heart fell to my toes. I stood up and moved toward the door. "Okay. But just to talk."

"Yes. Just to talk. After all these years that'll be so great."

Quietly, I opened the door. Mick and Officer Tripton looked around. "Yeah. It will. Sorry I sounded so mean." I stepped into the hallway and eased the door closed. My pulse was going a mile a minute. I jabbed my finger toward the phone, mouthing *It's him.* Officer Tripton's eyebrows shot up. He reached for his radio and flipped the sound off.

"It's okay," my father said. "I know it's hard hearing from me like this."

"So ... where are you?"

"On the third floor."

I nearly dropped the phone. *Where* on the third floor? I threw a panicked look down the hall.

"The third floor?" I locked wild eyes with the policeman. "So am I."

"In your Mom's room? I spotted the room awhile ago down a long hall — with two guards outside, one a policeman. It's why I called. I knew they'd never let me through."

My mouth opened, but no words came. He'd told the truth. He didn't have to do that. If he was trying to manipulate me into walking past those two guards — would he be that honest?

Of course he would. He had to convince me to make up an excuse to give them as to where I was going.

"Shaley?"

"Sorry. I'm here. I can just ... tell those guards outside I'm going to the nurse's station for something."

"Good. Get to the station and I'll tell you what to do."

He wants to keep me on the phone. So I won't talk to the policeman.

"Okay. Give me a minute to get out the door."

I lowered the phone and pointed down the hall. Officer Tripton nodded and tapped his radio. I backed up, hand over the phone's mouthpiece, until I was far enough away for him to speak into it quietly.

He gave me a thumbs up, gestured for Mick to stay put, then moved beside me.

My legs started to shake.

"Okay." I willed my voice to sound calm. "I'm walking toward the nurse's station." I fell quiet, heart ramming against my ribs. Officer Tripton's hand moved to hover over his gun. I looked away.

My father was going to die.

In front of the station, I stopped. "I'm here."

"Good. See the hall up and to your right? Take it. I'm in an empty room. Three sixty-seven."

That close. He was *that* close.

My throat tightened. All the childhood dreams of a long-lost father who loved me paraded mockingly through my mind. Every one of them ended here. In the next minute.

I felt like throwing up.

"Okay." I pointed for Officer Tripton, mouthing *around the corner — in a room.*

On legs I couldn't even feel, I moved forward. Turned up the corridor. Officer Tripton stayed by me. The first door on my right read 358. The room in which my father hid would be on my left.

My father.

Not far from that room a stairwell door opened. Four officers crept out of it, crouched low and soundless, guns drawn.

My right hand fisted against my stomach. Maybe they wouldn't shoot him here, in a hospital.

Of course they would. They'd be in a room away from other patients. Besides, if they threw open that door, and he drew a gun ...

What would I tell Mom? After seventeen years, her Gary had been here, *right here*, and I'd led the police to him, let them take him away.

Or worse, kill him.

Would she hate me?

Blood whooshed through my ears. Somehow my feet kept walking. I passed room 362.

"Where are you?" Franklin asked.

"Almost there."

"Any policemen around?"

"No."

Room 364 slid by. The four policemen drew near. One of them gestured to me — *where*?

My fingers cramped around the phone. I shot the officer a meaningful look. "Franklin. You said three sixty-seven?"

At the cue, Officer Tripton caught my arm. He slashed a hand through the air, waving me back.

"Yes," my father said.

I melted away from the policemen, back far enough that I'd be well out of the line of fire.

They advanced toward the door, guns ready. Five against one.

My trembling finger clicked off the call.

I couldn't breathe, couldn't move. Could only watch with the terrified eyes of a child who'd desperately longed to see her father face-to-face — and had now betrayed him.

43

Time spun out. In those final minutes a fireball of thoughts burned through my mind. I pictured Franklin Borden waiting on the other side of that door — for me. How stupid he was. Did he really think with one phone call, after I'd seen Jerry Brand kill two of my friends and try to kidnap me, I'd just walk past the men guarding me and put my life in his hands?

But he hadn't sounded stupid on the phone. And the Gary Donovon Mom had loved hadn't either.

The lead policeman reached the door. He checked over his shoulder to make sure that the other officers were ready.

And in that split second it hit me. My father wasn't stupid in his head. He *knew* better. He was just foolish in his heart. Because he so wanted to believe.

Like me. After all the years, even after seeing Tom and Bruce dead, after hearing Mom's story, right up to now — I still wanted to *believe*.

Gun ready, the officer planted his legs apart and reached for the door handle.

You didn't believe in someone like that, you didn't hold on to a dream that hard, when you wanted to hurt that person.

He just wants to see me. That was the truth. He meant it.

And I'd betrayed him. He was going to die.

The policeman threw open the door.

"No!" The scream tore from me, and I leapt forward, running, running. Knowing I wouldn't make it in time. Everything happened so fast. The first two officers rushed in, shouting, "On the ground, on the ground!" My father yelled. I screamed louder, barreling toward the door. The officer closest to me pivoted and jumped in my path. He held his gun low, away from me, and shoved me back.

More shouts from the room, all at once:

"On the ground!"

"He's got something in his hand!"

"Throw it down! Throw it *down*!"

I darted around the policeman. He scrambled to holster his gun so he could catch me. Too late. I rammed into the door jamb and ricocheted into the room.

"Stop! Don't kill him!"

My father struggled on the floor. Four officers crowded over him, capturing his legs, pulling out handcuffs. Everyone was shouting.

"*Stop!*"

"Be still!"

"Give me your hands!"

The last officer caught up with me and yanked me back. "Get *out* of here."

I burst into sobs. "Please, please, don't hurt him."

My father stilled. One officer snapped cuffs on his wrists. They hauled him to his feet.

He gazed at me.

Through blurry eyes I drank in the sight of him. He looked just like my mother had described. Still handsome. But his face had a hardness, as if life had worn him down. On that face I saw shock and betrayal. I also saw something else. Desperate hope.

"Shaley —"

"I'm sorry," I cried. "I didn't want to do it."

A red-faced and puffing officer clutched my father's arm. "When you went for that box you almost got yourself killed, man."

A gun. He *did* have a gun.

A flash went off behind me, and I jumped. Feet pounded away. I swung around to look out the door. Cat was running down the hall.

Stunned, I swiveled back toward my father. I didn't want to leave him. Then I thought of Cat and the photo — and what he'd do with it. Everyone in the world would see my father in handcuffs, surrounded by police.

"It's the photographer!" I tore out after Cat.

My feet sprinted down the hall, breath chugging from my open mouth. Cat veered around a corner.

"Shaley, stop!" a man behind me cried. A second later two policemen passed me. They sped around the corner, and I started to follow. Someone caught me from behind and pulled me back. I jerked my head around to see Officer Tripton. "Let me go, I have to catch him!"

"They'll get him, Shaley."

"Let me go!"

Shouts and scuffles sounded from around the corner. I yanked my arm away from Officer Tripton and rushed around. Three feet away, Cat struggled with the policemen on the floor. His camera lay on the ground. I couldn't stop in time. My foot caught one of Cat's flailing arms, and I went down on top of him.

All the fury I'd felt at Cat and all the anger and disappointment and hurt churning against my father poured out of me. I pounded Cat's head and face with both fists, screaming. "That's what you get for chasing me! For trying to blackmail me! That's what you get for hurting my mom! Stop it, just *stop* it!"

Strong arms pulled me off Cat and to my feet. Still my fists swung. Somebody pinned them to my sides. "It's okay, Shaley, we got him."

My chin dropped low, my chest heaving. I wanted to burst into tears but held them back.

Out the corner of my eye I saw Cat's camera by my feet. I kicked it as hard as I could. It skidded across the floor and smashed into the wall.

One of the policemen handcuffed Cat and yanked him to his feet. His eyes met mine, and he sneered. Hatred rolled off me in waves.

The policeman holding Cat's arm pulled him away. "Come on, buddy, let's go." He guided Cat toward the elevators some distance away.

Multiple footsteps filtered from around the corner. My father and the two other officers appeared. They were leading him away too. One of the officers held something in his hand, but I barely registered it. I could only stare at my father.

I'd done this. I'd sent him back to prison. Even though he deserved it, I just couldn't . . .

My vengeance against Cat melted. In its place all I could feel was deep, terrible sadness. I focused on the floor, tears flooding my eyes.

"Shaley." My father's voice shook. "It'll be okay."

I looked up at him in surprise. How could he say that?

He gestured with his chin toward the policeman's hand. "I brought something for you and your mom."

My gaze dropped to see a long, white box.

With a tight smile, the policeman held it out toward me.

For the longest time I could only stare at it, remembering Mom's story. Remembering Gary Donovon as she knew him. I thought of French class, and their first date. The day she sneaked over to his house. The night he got beat up. The gifts he'd sent her every month for the next eight years.

As if in a dream I reached out my hand and took the box. It felt smooth. Inviting. My throat choked up.

Blurry-eyed, I held the box in one hand and lifted off the lid.

Inside lay two white roses, each wrapped in green cellophane and tied with a red ribbon.

PART 14
Tuesday 2009

44

On Tuesday morning, my father visited Mom in her hospital room.

Seeing each other after all the years, the two of them deserved some privacy. I took a chair into the hall and sat with Wendell. On the outside I looked calm. But my insides jittered. So many unknowns. What would happen now? Could Mom and my father be friends? Would we ever see him again?

And what about the things we still didn't know? That night his house burned, why had he fled all the way out of state where she could never see him? Why didn't he ever call?

I'd been on the phone with Brittany for hours about it all. We hadn't been able to figure it out.

But he'd brought us white roses ...

The police guard had gone, no need for him now. Yesterday Detective Myner had questioned my father for hours at the Denver station only to decide they had nothing on the man. He appeared to be telling the truth about wanting to come just to see us. He'd never meant us any harm. He had no idea Jerry would hurt us. Jerry had gone crazy on his own. My father told the police about sharing a cell with Jerry, and they already knew those facts to be accurate.

In the end they let him go with a warning: "Watch yourself. Because we're watching *you*."

I witnessed the questioning through a one-way window. Detective Myner had been easy to convince about that. Not so with Mom and Ross — whom Mick had phoned as soon as I'd headed down the corridor with Officer Tripton. They finally gave in, and Ross went with me. Turned out to be a good thing. By the time the questioning was over, he believed my father too.

Busy watching my father, I hadn't been able to see Cat's interrogation. Didn't matter. He was in jail, that's what counted. Mom was pressing charges against him for assault, plus he'd be facing charges for the harassment in California and for breaking the restraining order. Mom also intended to sue Cat and *Cashing In* for her injuries. When she won — and she would — she'd put Cat and that rag magazine out of business for good.

The police had taken the film from Cat's smashed camera. He hadn't yet turned in the photo of me and Wendell. Even now as I sat with Wendell outside Mom's room, he didn't know the story that could have gone around the world about the two of us.

"That's really something." Wendell leaned forward, powerful hands clasped between his knees. His short black hair was perfectly gelled straight up, as usual. "Your dad coming back after all this time."

"Yeah. I know."

He glanced at me. "Kinda dumb thing you did, Shaley, running into the middle of all those policemen and guns."

As if Ross hadn't told me the same thing a million times. I thought of his warning to me yesterday — *don't go running off by yourself, Shaley.* Well, I hadn't been by myself. I'd had five policemen around me.

"I know. I just ... lost my head. I was so afraid they'd shoot him."

Minutes ticked by in silence. I got up and wandered the width of the hall, back and forth, back and forth.

"How do you sit here all day, Wendell? This would drive me *crazy.*"

He grunted. "Not the funnest part of my job. Fortunately, I don't do it for this long very often."

I waited out there for over two hours.

Finally the door to Mom's room opened. My father stuck his head out. "Shaley, could you come in now?"

Heart in my throat, I followed him inside.

Mom's bed was cranked almost straight up. She wore her own clothes this morning. The pain hadn't lessened much, but knowing my father was coming, she'd forced herself into the bathroom to clean up with a nurse's help. The bump on her head was a dark purple.

In the presence of both my parents, I felt suddenly shy. I didn't know how to be with a mother and father in the same room.

"Shaley." Mom beckoned me to a chair by her bed. I sat down, my father standing beside me. "We've talked." Mom smiled at him. "I want you to know that everything's all right."

I looked questioningly from her to him. "Okay."

Mom gave me a weary smile. "There are still some things you need to hear."

Oh, so many things. I nodded.

"Gary, tell her."

Gary. She still called him Gary.

"Let me get the other seat." My father headed for the door. He stepped into the hall and returned, carrying the chair. I watched his every move, unable to speak. He put it down and sat facing me.

"Now I can really look at you."

I swallowed hard.

He took a deep breath. "Your mom said she's told you about us."

My chin went up and down the slightest bit. I could feel my heart knocking as I gazed into my father's face.

"I want to tell you the truth about the night my house burned. It's not what you were told, or what I told your mom at the time. The Westrock gang didn't set that fire. *I* did."

My mouth dropped open.

"They had me, Shaley. Westrock gang members lived all over Southern California, all over the state. There was nowhere I could go to get out from under them except far away. And if I stayed,

I'd be their puppet. I'd *have* to do what they said — to keep my grandmother and your mom safe. Until the police caught me. And then I'd have to take the rap all by myself. A snitch in jail would be killed." He stopped for a moment, as if gathering the strength to go on. "Even if I ran far, Bart would have people looking for me. Because he'd have to save face, you understand? He couldn't let other members see he'd let someone slip from his grasp."

I stared at him, remembering the words he'd insisted that Mom say to Bart. *After you burned down Gary's house, he and his grandmother left the state. He's never coming back. And nobody's going to the police. You tell him that, and he'll leave you alone.*

Sudden understanding locked in my mind. "You burned down your house so Bart would save face. He could tell everyone *he* did it — he forced you out of town."

"That's right."

I shook my head. How *awful*. To forfeit everything he owned, everything his grandmother owned. To know he'd have to run with nothing but the clothes on his back ...

My mother's description of how he looked that night came back to me. *His eyes told the truth. If he faltered now, if he hesitated one little bit, he'd lose his resolve completely — and stay.*

Gary Donovon *burned his own house*, knowing he'd have to leave immediately. Leave the girl he loved. In order to keep her safe.

"But why didn't you call?" I burst. "Mom could have come to see you in Arizona. You wouldn't have to be apart forever!"

Pain quivered across his face. "You don't know how much I wanted to. Day after day, night after night, I thought about your mom. I was so lonely. I missed her so much, missed my home. But I couldn't risk it. As long as she didn't know where I was, never talked to me, there was nothing Bart and his friends would want with her. After such a sacrifice of burning my own home, how could I gamble with her safety? So I reached out the one way I could. I sent her the roses."

"But as time passed you didn't think — maybe now it will be okay?"

"How could I know when that would be? And as time went on, I knew your mom's life would have gone on too. Remember, I didn't know about you. And I had my grandmother to take care of. She got a lot worse after that night. She lingered for nine years, then passed away. After that I . . . lost myself."

A lump sat in my throat. I tore my eyes away from him and looked to Mom. She nodded. In that small motion I read a huge meaning. *Yes, you can believe him. I do.*

"So . . . Shaley, will you forgive me?" he asked. "Can we start from here?"

"But you lied to me. You told me you didn't know I was here at the hospital. But you did."

He looked at his feet. "I know. I'm sorry. I was so afraid you wouldn't believe that I didn't mean you any harm. I was afraid you'd think I was stalking you."

That made sense, but still . . . Too many years had gone by. Too many disappointments. Lying was no way to start talking to somebody. My mouth firmed, and I looked my father square in the eye. "Don't do that again. If you want me to trust you, if you want Mom to trust you, you *can't* lie to us."

He nodded solemnly. "You're right. Here's my promise — I won't lie to either of you. Ever again." He swallowed hard, and his eyes glimmered. "Prison changes a man. I have to learn how to live on the outside again. But I can put that behind me forever. I can live a good life, like I did before. And as I do that, I want to be a part of *your* life, Shaley."

My heart turned over as I gazed again at the man before me. The father I'd waited so long to know, had begged God as a child to bring to me. My thoughts flicked to yesterday, huddled and crying in the bathroom. *I'm ready to give myself to you, God,* I'd prayed, *but I'm not even sure how to start . . .*

On the phone my father had told me people aren't all black and white. That we live in shades of gray. "I'm asking you for forgiveness," he'd said. Now he was asking again.

This is how it starts, isn't it, God? With forgiveness.

My mouth trembled. I glanced at Mom, then leaned forward to take my father's hands. "Yes, I forgive you. And I'm so glad you've come back." My voice broke. I squeezed his hands. "I've waited for you for a very long time."

45

That afternoon the band members would be going back to Southern California on their chartered plane. Mom couldn't stand to stay behind.

"I'm already going crazy in this room," she told Ross as he stood, arms folded, by her bed. My father was in the cafeteria, getting something to eat. "There's nothing more the doctors need to do to me, and I can take pills for the pain. Just get me out of here, Ross. I want to go home."

Home. My vision blurred. Brittany. Our house. My own bed. Please, please, yes. So much had happened in the last four days. I was exhausted. Like Mom, I just wanted to go *home*.

"Rayne." Ross patted her cast. "You want to get out of here, you know I'll make it happen."

I leaned my head back and gazed at the ceiling. *Thank you, God. Thank you!*

Mom nodded. She raised her chin and gave him a Rayne O'Connor look. The searing, confident rock star eyes her fans knew so well. "We need three seats."

"Three?" Ross raised his eyebrows.

"One for Gary."

"Rayne, come on."

Mom looked at me as she spoke. "Ross, he has to rebuild a life somewhere. All we're doing is giving him a ride to Southern California."

"Where he can be near *you*."

"And me," I jumped in. "I want to give him a chance."

Ross shook his head. "He's not the person you knew all those years ago, Rayne."

"No. But neither am I."

"You'll regret this."

Mom smiled to herself. "I don't think so."

I caught her hand. No, she wouldn't. Neither would I. Prison might have hardened my father's face, but his heart was the same. He just needed to get back to the man he used to be.

Ross heaved a sigh. "Okay, Rayne. It's your life. Three seats."

Happiness burst through me until I could hardly contain it. Whirling, I snatched up the cell phone on my bed. I pressed and held a well-used button. My best friend answered on the second ring. "Shaley, what's going on?"

"Brittany, I'm coming home! *Today!*"

"Yay!" she squealed.

My voice choked up. I took a shaky breath — and spoke the words I'd dreamed of saying for years.

"And guess what else. I'm bringing my father with me."

These discussion questions can be used in a book club (a mother – daughter book club, a teen book club) or even as questions to use with friends also reading this book.

1. In the opening of the book, Shaley manages to keep herself together, even after all that happened to her in *Always Watching*. How do you think she's finding the strength? When hard things happen to you, where do you find the strength to deal with everything?

2. Shaley hates and fears the paparazzi because of her experiences with them. Do you think she's being weak in this fear, given the fact that paparazzi have been following the band for years?

3. Was Rayne right to do what she did when she saw Cat? What would you have done?

4. Brittany is the first person Shaley talks to about what Jerry whispered in her ear before he died. Was Shaley right not to tell her mom or the police? Would you have told your best friend first?

5. In Chapter 9, Shaley thinks, *For the first time it occurred to me that maybe some good could come out of this terrible accident.* She and her mother may now be able to talk about Shaley's father, instead of fighting. Have you ever seen good come out of a terrible situation? How long after the bad event did you realize good had resulted from it?

6. Was Rayne right to not tell Shaley everything about her father all these years? What would you have done?

7. What did the story about Rayne and Gary teach you about real love? What about the love between Gary and his grandmother?

8. If you were Shaley, would you have tried to get past the bodyguard to find Cat on your own? Would you have done it differently, and how?

9. How hard of a time do you think Rayne had, trying to raise a baby at the age of seventeen without the father?

10. What did you think of Franklin Borden as you read his chapters? What did you think Franklin was planning to do?

11. In Chapter 42, Shaley's father tells her, "People aren't all black and white. We're all shades of gray. Even a good person can make a mistake." Do you believe that? Why?

12. Throughout *Always Watching* and *Last Breath*, Shaley is slowly drawn closer to God. Yet in *Last Breath*, while she is crying in the bathroom, she thinks, *I'm ready to give myself to you, God, but I'm not even sure how to start.* At the end of the book she thinks, *This is how it starts, isn't it, God? With forgiveness.* Do you agree with that? Is that true for everyone, or just for Shaley because of her circumstances?

13. How would you advise your friend or your daughter to give herself to God?

14. What were your favorite parts in this story?

15. How is Shaley most like you? How is she different?

16. What do you think will happen between Rayne and Gary?

Carter House Girls Series
from Melody Carlson

Mix six teenage girls and one '60s fashion icon (retired, of course) in an old Victorian-era boarding home. Add boys and dating, a little high school angst, and throw in a Kate Spade bag or two ... and you've got the Carter House Girls, Melody Carlson's new chick lit series for young adults!

Mixed Bags
Book One

Stealing Bradford
Book Two

Homecoming Queen
Book Three

Viva Vermont!
Book Four

Lost in Las Vegas
Book Five

New York Debut
Book Six

Spring Breakdown
Book Seven

Last Dance
Book Eight

Available in stores and online!

ZONDERVAN®
.com

Sweet Seasons by Debbie Viguié!

Join Candace Thompson on a sweet, lighthearted, and honest romp through the friendships, romances, family and friend dramas, and faith discoveries that make a girl's life as full as it can be.

Summer of Cotton Candy

Fall of Candy Corn

Winter of Candy Canes

Spring of Candy Apples

Also available in ebook versions.

Available in stores and online!

ZONDERVAN®
.com

Teen Study Bible

As an on-the-go teen, you're moving fast. God is moving faster! Totally revised, this bestselling Bible will help you discover the eternal truths of God's Word and apply them to the issues you face today.

Features include:

- We Believe—Unpacks the Apostles' Creed to reveal the biblical foundation of faith
- Panorama—Keeps the big picture of each book of the Bible in view
- Tip-in Pages—Explain ancient ruins, foreign languages, music, and more
- Key Indexes—Help with in-depth Bible study
- To the Point—Reveals what the Bible says about pressing issues
- Dear Jordan—Offers biblical advice for teens
- Instant Access—Tells what God says to you personally
- Q&A—Tests your knowledge of Bible trivia
- Bible Promises—Highlight Bible verses worth remembering
- Book Introductions—Provide an overview for each book of the Bible
- Complete NIV Text—The most read, most trusted Bible translation

Pick up a copy today at your favorite bookstore!

The Rayne Tour

by Brandilyn Collins and Amberly Collins!

A suspenseful three-book series for young adults written by bestselling author Brandilyn Collins and her daughter, Amberly. The series is about the daughter of a rock star, life on the road, and her search for her real father.

Always Watching

Book One

This daughter of a rock star has it all —until murder crashes her world.

Last Breath

Book Two

With his last breath, a dying man whispered four stunning words into Shaley O'Connor's ear. Should she believe them?

Final Touch

Book Three

Shaley O'Connor is kidnapped minutes before the long-awaited wedding of her mother and once-estranged father.

Pick up a copy today at your favorite bookstore!

Violet Dawn

Brandilyn Collins

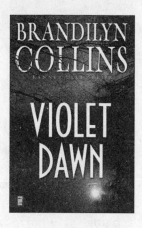

Something sinuous in the water brushed against Paige's knee. She jerked her leg away.

What was that? She rose to a sitting position, groped around with her left hand.

Fine wisps wound themselves around her fingers.

Hair?

She yanked backward, but the tendrils clung. Something solid bumped her wrist.

Paige gasped. With one frantic motion she shook her arm free, grabbed the side of the hot tub, and heaved herself out.

Paige Williams slips into her hot tub in the blackness of night — and finds herself face to face with death.

Alone, terrified, fleeing a dark past, Paige must make an unthinkable choice.

In *Violet Dawn*, hurtling events and richly drawn characters collide in a breathless story of murder, the need to belong, and faith's first glimmer. One woman's secrets unleash an entire town's pursuit, and the truth proves as elusive as the killer in their midst.

Pick up a copy today at your favorite bookstore!

Coral Moon

Brandilyn Collins

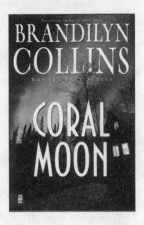

The figure remained still as stone. Leslie couldn't even detect a breath.

Spider fingers teased the back of her neck.

Leslie's feet rooted to the pavement. She dropped her gaze to the driveway, seeking ... what? Spatters of blood? Footprints? She saw nothing. Honed through her recent coverage of crime scene evidence, the testimony at last month's trial, the reporter in Leslie spewed warnings: Notice everything, touch nothing.

Leslie Williams hurries out to her car on a typical workday morning—and discovers a dead body inside. Why was the corpse left for her to find? And what is the meaning of the message pinned to its chest?

In *Coral Moon*, the senseless murder of a beloved Kanner Lake citizen spirals the small Idaho town into a terrifying glimpse of spiritual forces beyond our world. What appears true seems impossible.

Or is it?

Pick up a copy today at your favorite bookstore!

Crimson Eve

Brandilyn Collins, Bestselling Author of Violet Dawn

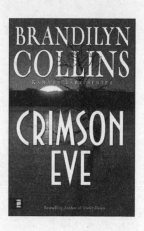

Carla stared at the gun and David Thornby — or whatever his name was. Her mind fissured, one side pleading this was some sick joke, the other knowing it was not. Her throat ran dry, air backing up in her lungs. She swallowed.

"Please. You must have the wrong person. There's no reason for someone to want me dead. I don't have any enemies."

"Then you'd best rethink your friends."

Realtor Carla Radling shows an "English gentleman" a lakeside estate — and finds herself facing a gun. Who has hired this assassin to kill her, and why?

Forced on the run, Carla must uncover the scathing secrets of her past. Secrets that could destroy some very powerful people. Perhaps even change the face of a nation ...

Crimson Eve is book three in the Kanner Lake Series. Set in a small lakeshore town in pristine northern Idaho, this series combines suspense and fast-paced action with intriguing, well-crafted characters and many an unexpected twist.

Pick up a copy today at your favorite bookstore!

Amber Morn

Brandilyn Collins

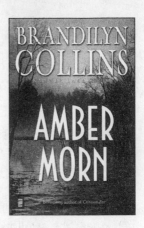

The whole thing couldn't have taken more than sixty seconds.

Bailey hung on to the counter, dazed. If she let go, she'd collapse — and the twitching fingers of one of the gunmen would pull a trigger. The rest of her group huddled in frozen shock.

Dear God, tell me this is a dream …

The shooter's teeth clenched. "Anybody who moves is dead."

On a beautiful Saturday morning the nationally read "Scenes and Beans" bloggers gather at Java Joint for a special celebration. Chaos erupts when three gunmen burst in and take them all hostage. One person is shot and dumped outside.

Police Chief Vince Edwards must negotiate with the desperate trio. The gunmen insist on communicating through the "comments" section of the blog — so all the world can hear their story. What they demand, Vince can't possibly provide. But if he doesn't, over a dozen beloved Kanner Lake citizens will die …

Pick up a copy today at your favorite bookstore!